HIGH HURDLES

DJ's Challenge

High Hurdles

1. *Olympic Dreams*
2. *DJ's Challenge*

Golden Filly Series

1. *The Race*
2. *Eagle's Wings*
3. *Go for the Glory*
4. *Kentucky Dreamer*
5. *Call for Courage*
6. *Shadow Over San Mateo*
7. *Out of the Mist*
8. *Second Wind*
9. *Close Call*
10. *The Winner's Circle*

HIGH HURDLES

DJ's Challenge

LAURAINE SNELLING

BETHANY HOUSE PUBLISHERS
MINNEAPOLIS, MINNESOTA 55438

Cover illustration by Paul Casale

Published by Bethany House Publishers
A Ministry of Bethany Fellowship, Inc.
11300 Hampshire Avenue South
Minneapolis, Minnesota 55438

Printed in the United States of America.

Library of Congress Cataloging-in-Publication Data

Snelling, Lauraine.
    DJ's challenge / Lauraine Snelling.
        p.   cm. — (High hurdles ; bk. 2)
    Summary: A new job for her mother and a possible move to another city threaten to part DJ from her horse.

    [1. Moving, Household—Fiction. 2. Horses—Fiction.]
I. Title. II. Series: Snelling, Lauraine. High hurdles ; bk. 2.
PZ7.S677Dj   1995
[Fic]—dc20   95-9624
ISBN 1-55661-506-X   CIP
                                                                AC

To my mentor and friend

Colleen Reece

who's given me tools
to make writing easier and
encouragement to keep
growing on.

LAURAINE SNELLING is a full-time writer who has authored a number of books, both fiction and nonfiction, as well as written articles for a wide range of magazines and weekly features for local newspapers. She also teaches writing courses and trains people in speaking skills. She and her husband, Wayne, have two grown children and make their home in California.

Her lifelong love of horses began at age five with a pony named Polly and continued with Silver, Kit, Rowdy, and her daughter's horse, Cimeron, which starred in her first children's book, *Tragedy on the Toutle*.

1

BEING GROUNDED WAS THE PITS. Even though it *was* her own fault for almost running away. She *had* come back. They hadn't had to call the police or anything. Darla Jean Randall, DJ to anyone who wanted to remain on her good side, stared at the telephone and tried to forget the dumb things she'd done. She couldn't even call her best friend, Amy Yamamoto, since the phone was off limits, too. Amy could be dying from chicken pox for all DJ knew—as if her mother cared.

Now . . . if someone called her, would it be okay to talk? DJ shook her head, her wavy, golden ponytail slapping from side to side. She'd never been grounded like this before. And the few times she had been, Gran, her mother's mother, had been there to clarify the rules. Or bend them.

The thought of Gran turned the ache into a pain, one that seemed to surround her heart and squeeze. Last Saturday—three days and twelve hours ago—Gran had married soon-to-be-retired Police Captain Joe Crowder. Right now they were somewhere off the coast of Mexico, living it up on a honeymoon cruise.

DJ pushed herself out of Gran's winged recliner and

scuffed her bare feet all the way up the stairs to her bedroom. She crawled into bed and pulled the covers up over her head. Maybe it was a good thing school was starting pretty soon after all.

Pedaling her bike past Amy's house in the early morning brought on another pang of loneliness, as if the again empty house she'd left behind weren't enough. *Is this what latchkey kids felt like? Am I a latchkey kid?* She fingered the key she wore on a chain around her neck. She snorted and pedaled harder. At fourteen she was pretty grown-up to be called a kid of any kind.

Amy had to get over the chicken pox in the next couple days. Then at least they could talk on the way back and forth to the Academy where they both worked. Maybe if she could shoot the breeze with Amy, she wouldn't miss Gran so much.

The horses nickering down the aisle brought the first smile of the morning to her mouth. She put two fingers between her lips and blew, the whistle echoing off the rafters of the low red barn. The nickers turned to whinnies, and where the stalls' upper doors had been opened, her equine friends nodded to her.

"Hey, you about broke my eardrums." Hilary Jones, one of the older riders whom DJ looked up to, strode out of the tack room, English saddle over her arm.

"Sorry." The grin DJ shot her made the apology an out-and-out fib.

"Sure you are. And so are all your friends. You riding today?"

DJ shook her head.

"Sorry."

DJ dug in the sack of carrots she kept in the stable refrigerator. "That's okay. At least I won't be grounded for the rest of my life."

"Just seems like it?"

"Yep." DJ picked up a bucket of brushes and combs. "I gotta get to work. With Amy home sick, I never get a break."

"I'll help you after I finish practicing. We're still having trouble with the square oxer. Prince keeps dropping his back feet before the second bar, so either he doesn't get it or I come down on him midfence." As Hilary headed for her horse's stall, she called over her shoulder, "Hang in there."

"Right." DJ hoisted her bucket to check to see if it contained a hoof-pick. If only Diablo were here. But the fiery chestnut gelding she'd been training and showing for the Ortegas had moved with them to Texas. There had been too many changes in her life lately.

She started down the line. Each horse got a carrot snack, a heavy dose of loving, and a thorough grooming. DJ clipped them on the hot walker while she shoveled out the dirty shavings.

"Easy, fella," she cautioned a rambunctious school horse. "You'll get your workout in a bit." She snapped him to the crossties since he had a habit of sneaking in a nip or two. "You just think you own the world, that's all." She tapped his foot with the pick. The horse stood there. She ran her hand down the back of his foreleg and pulled at his fetlock. He snorted.

DJ stood upright and clamped her hands on her hips. "You would pick today to be difficult." He turned to gaze at her. She could swear she saw an imp dancing in his eye. He nosed her back pocket. "No way. Bad horses don't get second treats. Now give me that foot."

This time, the horse let her raise the hoof and rest it on her bent knee so she could pick out the compacted manure and shavings. She could feel his breath on her rear. "You bite me, and you'll be dog food for sure."

She moved to the rear hoof. It took three tries before he let her pick it up. "What's the matter with you, get up on the wrong side of the stall or something?" She glanced up to check his ears. Sure enough, they were laid back. "All right, knock it off." She felt him relax. Only now he leaned his weight on her. By the time she finished, she could feel sweat trickling down between her shoulder blades. She trotted the problem horse out to the hot walker and, after snapping him in place, gave him a slap on the rump. "Work off some of that orneriness before your riders come."

"You want to ride Gray Bar?" James, the former academy terror who'd only recently become DJ's friend, stopped her dog trot to the next stall.

"I wish." DJ wiped a hand across her damp forehead.

"Still grounded?"

"Right. You okay?"

James shrugged. "'Bout the same. I've been accepted at West Virginia Military Academy. Great, huh?" The look on his face said it was anything but.

"When do you leave?"

"I'm not sure. Too soon—or not soon enough if my mom and dad have anything to say about it." He turned and continued brushing his gray Arab filly.

DJ stroked the filly's broad cheeks and dished face. "She is so beautiful." Gray Bar nosed DJ's pocket. "Sorry, girl. I'm all out of treats."

James brushed his way to the filly's rump. "If you

wanted to ride her, I wouldn't tell."

DJ could get away with it. Bridget Sommersby, owner of the Academy, wasn't here; she had a meeting somewhere this morning. And none of the other student workers would rat on her. DJ wanted to ride Gray Bar so bad she could feel it like a toothache.

She sucked in a deep breath. "Thanks, James. But I gave my word. Not riding for a couple weeks never killed anyone." She could hear Gran's voice in her ear. *A real lady always keeps her word.* While being a true southern gentlewoman like Gran was not at the top of DJ's priorities, she knew keeping her word was a mark of a Christian, too. And that *was* important.

"See ya, I gotta get back to work." By the time she'd finished, the sun blazed well past the sky's zenith. She could hear Bridget giving instructions to a class in the jumping ring; a class DJ would be part of if she hadn't been grounded. Megs, Bridget's mare, now retired from the show and jumping ring, needed a good workout. But jumping classes, like nearly everything else that could be called fun, were forbidden while DJ was grounded. Why, oh why, had she panicked and run like that?

DJ swung aboard her bike and pedaled toward home—and an empty house. If she hadn't been in such a hurry to escape it that morning, she could have packed a lunch. There was always tack to clean. But the rumblings from her midsection nearly drowned out the singing of her tires on the pavement.

How come an empty house even smelled lonely? She checked the machine for messages—none. After tossing a pound of frozen hamburger in the sink to thaw for tonight's tacos, she stuck her nose in the refrigerator. Baloney sandwich? Nah. Tuna? Yuck. Grilled cheese? She pulled the block of cheddar from the door and cut off a chunk. The groan and then hum of the fridge made her jump.

When she ambled back into the kitchen again, evening had fallen. Chores, drawing, and making dinner had used up most of her time. DJ glared at the silent telephone hanging on the wall. *Ring, you stupid machine.* She paced into Gran's studio, which replaced what would have been the family room in most homes. Another silent phone took up part of a lamp table. Silent like the entire house. A house that, until now, had always rung with Gran's chuckles and her hymns on the stereo. Always smelled good from something baking or cooking, and always wrapped comforting arms around those who lived there. Always. Except now. At least the tacos DJ had made for dinner canceled the empty smell. Her mother did like tacos if she hadn't already eaten.

DJ glanced up at the clock. Her mother should be home from class pretty soon. Lindy Randall was on her way to a Master's degree, earned after her day job selling guns, flak vests, and other supplies to police departments. Most of Lindy's life was spent working, traveling for work, studying, and dressing in knockout clothes. She claimed her expensive wardrobe helped her make a better living for her family—or at least that was her excuse for spending so much money on the latest styles.

DJ looked down at her grungy jeans. The horses at the Academy where she worked and rode didn't care if her jeans had a hole in one knee and smelled like a stable. In fact, they liked it. One shoulder of her navy blue T-shirt sported horse slobber to prove it. She glanced in the sink. She needed to put stuff in the dishwasher and wipe down the counters.

"The sprinklers. Gotta get that done first." Even her voice sounded loud in the empty house. Bare feet slapped across the cedar deck to the backyard, where she turned on the sprinklers and stood watching to make sure the lawn and flower beds were getting their needed soaking. Now that evening had come to the Pleasant Hill, California, community, less water would be wasted in the heat. Gran and DJ had spent hours together learning how they could best help the environment.

How come everything pointed back to Gran?

Think of Major! A month after Joe and Gran came back, Joe would retire from the mounted patrol. His horse, Major, would retire with him. But Major wouldn't be put out to pasture. He would belong to DJ. Joe said the $380 she'd saved from the pony parties and all her other money-raising schemes would be enough to pay for him.

DJ hurried back into the house and up the stairs to her horse-decorated bedroom. A picture of Joe on Major, both in uniform, perched in the middle of her desk. DJ flicked on the lamp. The white blaze down the blood bay's face and his two white socks gleamed in the light. Joe said Major was the best horse and friend anyone could have. And he liked to jump.

DJ raised her eyes to the poster on the wall. The five entwined Olympic gold rings shone above the horse and rider jumping a triple. She repeated her daily affirmation. "One day I, DJ, will jump in the Olympics." Grabbing her sketch pad, she flopped down on the bed. Within a heartbeat the drawing she'd been working on that afternoon absorbed her concentration.

"Darla Jean Randall!"

DJ's gaze flew first to the clock—it was after nine—and then to the window. It was nearly dark. Where had the time gone? She leaped off her bed and down the stairs. The kitchen! She'd left the kitchen a mess.

"Hi, Mom."

Lindy Randall stood at the oak dining room table, sorting the mail with one hand and rubbing her forehead with the other.

Uh-oh, that meant a headache. DJ closed her eyes. Not a good night to have left a mess.

Lindy dropped the envelopes onto the table and used the fingertips of both hands to rub her temples. "You'd think you could do the little bit I ask of you without being reminded." The words came out hard and biting.

"But, Mom—"

"No *buts*. You made the mess, you clean it up. That doesn't seem too much to ask."

"I thought—"

"No, you didn't. You never think, you just act."

"I made dinner for both of us." DJ reared back at the word *never*.

"You know how I hate a messy kitchen."

"Yeah, well, excuse me. I thought maybe you'd like something to eat when you got home. Sorry I'm not Gran."

"You don't have to bring Gran into this. Your thoughtlessness is between you and me. I raised you to—"

"You never raised me. Gran did. You're never home—you couldn't raise a flea." DJ spun around and headed for the kitchen.

"Darla Jean, you can't talk to me like that."

DJ threw the pans in the sink, the clatter making as angry a sound as her stomping.

Better cool it, DJ, she warned herself. But the fires raging at her mother's accusations refused to bank.

A glass shattering against the cast-iron skillet in the sink brought her up short. A line of blood trickled from a spot on the back of her hand where a sliver of glass had embedded itself.

Say you're sorry! "I'm not sorry," she muttered into the back of her hand as she sucked the blood out of the wound. She could feel the piece of glass with her tongue.

"If you can't be polite, you can just go to your room."

"I'm cleaning up the kitchen, can't you tell?" DJ let the door of the dishwasher clang open. How would she get the glass out? Blood dripped down over her fingers. Oh, great. What had she done? Cut a vein or something?

Gingerly she picked out the pieces of glass in the bottom of the sink and dropped them in the trash. She couldn't apply pressure to the wound to make it stop bleeding. She ran cold water from the tap over her hand. Pink blood stained the white enamel. Maybe she'd bleed to death—then she'd find out if her mother really cared. At least there'd be no one around to leave a mess.

The cut stung like fury. "Stop bleeding, you stupid thing." All the while she tossed stuff in the trash, put dishes in the dishwasher, and scrubbed the frying pan. "I shoulda just had peanut butter. Why'd I try to make something *she* likes? Never does any good anyway." Her mutterings were drowned out by the running water.

The blood kept dripping.

She wiped up the counters. Each swipe of the dishcloth wiped up watery drops of blood. How long did it take to bleed to death? Could she be so lucky?

2

"DARLA JEAN RANDALL, what have you done now?"

"Cut myself, as if you care." DJ leaned over the sink. Wasn't she losing an awful lot of blood?

"Let me look at that." Mom grasped DJ's hand, carefully keeping it over the sink. "How did it happen?"

"Broken glass. There's still a piece in there." DJ wanted to yank her hand out of her mother's, but the warm contact felt good.

"Here." Lindy pulled off several paper towels and bunched them under the dripping hand. "Let's go up to the bathroom where the light's better. Maybe we can see the glass then and get it out with tweezers." Her voice still hadn't lost its hard edge, but at least she wasn't yelling.

DJ bit her lip against the pain. How come such a little cut could bleed so much?

Upstairs in the bathroom with good light, a magnifying glass, and steady hands, Mom lifted the glass sliver free and, with both thumbs holding the cut open, sluiced water over it for several minutes.

DJ squinted her eyes against the sting. She would not

17

complain—no matter what. Letting her anger rule her like that made her feel like sticking her head in the toilet bowl and flushing. *Why can't I control my temper? What's the matter with me? I pray about it and pray about it, and look what happens.* She didn't dare glance up because she didn't want to catch her mother's gaze in the mirror.

"Here, put some pressure on this while I get out the Band-Aids." Lindy looked up just as DJ did, and, sure enough, their eyes locked in the mirror.

"Oh, DJ, what are we going to do?" Lindy put an arm around her daughter's shoulders and squeezed.

"I'm sorry I left the mess and then mouthed off. I hate myself when I do that."

"Join the club. Just because I had a headache was no reason to light into you." She finished drying DJ's hand. "How's it feel?"

"Hurts." DJ lifted her fingers from the cut so her mother could apply antibiotic ointment and a bandage. "Thanks for getting the glass out. I thought I might bleed to death or something."

"Thought it or wished it?"

"Huh?"

"You heard me. I remember being fourteen and fighting with my mother. Sometimes you remind me so much of me that it scares the bejeebers out of me."

"You used to fight with Gran?" DJ couldn't believe her ears. "Gran never fights with anyone. She says a lady never raises her voice."

"Gran wasn't always as genteel as she is now. But then, I really knew how to push her buttons. Kinda like you do mine."

DJ smoothed the ends of the tan plastic strip down with her forefinger.

"When you get a southern woman riled, you've got a real problem on your hands." Lindy rubbed her forehead again. "I need to change and—"

"Mom, you've got blood on your suit." DJ touched the spots on the lower sleeve of the cream silk. "I'm sorry."

"It'll come out. How about getting me a glass of water and two aspirins? If your hand works now, that is."

DJ looked up in time to catch a smile lifting the corners of her mother's mouth. Her mother was teasing her. Actually trying to make a joke. And after a big fight, too. *Maybe miracles really do happen.*

DJ took the stairs two at a time both down and up. She'd finish cleaning the kitchen later.

"Thanks, dear." Lindy swallowed the tablets and collapsed on the bed.

"You need anything else?" DJ stuck her hands in her pockets.

"You wouldn't have a spare million lying around anywhere, would you?"

"Sorry."

"Good-night, then. Guess I'll just try to sleep this thing off."

DJ bent down and dropped a kiss on her mother's cheek. The fragrance of expensive perfume filled her nose. " 'Night." DJ turned at the door. "Thanks for fixing my hand."

"You're welcome." Eyes closed, Lindy waggled her fingers from their place on top of the covers.

DJ fell asleep promising both herself and her heavenly Father she wouldn't lose her temper like that again. One thing she was grateful for, her restrictions hadn't been extended. Was that thanks to the cut? Probably a good thing she hadn't bled to death after all. "When I have kids," she promised herself, "I'm not gonna say 'you always' or 'you never,' like Mom does. Nobody does things 'always' or 'never.' "

In the morning she found a note on the counter.

"Sorry for the way I blew up at you. How about going out for dinner tonight; maybe we can do some real talking. I should be home early. Love, Mom."

DJ read the note a second and third time. *Her* mother apologizing? On one hand she felt she could touch the stars, on the other, an ant belly would be higher off the floor than her feelings. She grabbed a couple of food bars and an apple, stuffing them into her backpack along with a can of soda. At least now she could stay at the Academy longer. The house could stay empty all day.

"Bridget wants to see you," Hilary called when DJ walked into the barn.

"What for?"

"How should I know?"

"Oh, okay, thanks." DJ threw the words over her shoulder, already halfway to the office.

Bridget Sommersby, Academy owner and former Olympic contender, sat at her oak desk behind piles of papers, magazines, file folders, and a frayed girth strap. The pained look on her face and the ledger in front of her said she was working on the books. Her feelings about the bookkeeping end of her business were well known to all who knew her.

"You wanted me?" DJ knew that if she was in trouble, bookkeeping time was not a good time to get called on the carpet. This was worse than the principal's office.

"Hi, DJ, sit down. You saved me." The smile on Bridget's square-jawed face told DJ she was not in trouble. Bridget stuck the pencil she'd been using into her slicked-into-a-bun blond hair. "How are things going?"

DJ sank down into the wooden chair by the desk. "Going."

"That bad, huh?" At DJ's nod, Bridget pulled the pencil back out and tapped the eraser on the desk. "How much longer do you have in jail?"

DJ felt her heavy mood begin to lighten. "A week. Guess I'll live through it."

"Not riding is rough." Bridget leaned back in her swivel chair. She let the pause lengthen while she studied DJ over the tops of her horn-rimmed half glasses. "How would you like Patches back?" She raised a hand to suggest DJ not leap out of her chair. DJ settled back on the edge of her seat. "Hilary has already started classes at Diablo Valley College and just does not have the time to train and work anything but her own mount right now. So, while I agree with your mother on the importance of discipline, as an employer, I need you to work Patches. I take it this would not cause you unhappiness?"

"Not in the least." DJ could respond formally when needed. But she couldn't disguise the bounce of pleasure that rocked the chair.

"Fine, here is the training program I have set up." Bridget handed a sheet of instructions across the desk. "Hopefully Amy will be back soon, because I would like you to work with Patches an hour a day at least—for now. His owners want him ready for their young son to ride. Mrs. Johnson plans to take lessons once a week on him, too, after school starts."

"Wouldn't the boy do better on a pony at first? Maybe like Bandit? Patches is pretty big." DJ sat on her hands so she wouldn't bite her nails.

"True." Bridget nodded. "That is a good suggestion. I will talk to the McDougalls. Maybe exchange some board for using Bandit as a schooling horse." The phone at her right hand rang. "Talk to you later."

DJ was out the door almost before Bridget answered "hello." She got to ride again! It felt as though she hadn't been on a horse for a hundred years or more.

She rushed through her assigned stalls, making sure each horse got its required care, but not spending her normal amount of time scratching ears and giving love pats. She left Patches till last.

"Howdy, Patches, old boy. You ready for some training?" The big dark bay snuffled her hair, then rubbed his forehead against her shoulder. "You're just a sweetie, you know that?" DJ leaned down to retrieve two brushes from the bucket, one for each hand. "Let's get you all shined up and ready to work." She kept up a running monologue, her tongue moving in rhythm with her hands while she brushed, combed his tail, and picked hooves. The white splotch between his eyes gleamed white in the dim light.

"You're going to make a real flashy show horse someday, you know that?" She finished by wiping down his face with a soft brush. She dropped the pick and brushes back in her bucket and set it outside the stall door. Once he was saddled and bridled, she led him out and trotted him over to the ring, to mount inside the gate. Just swinging her leg over the Western saddle and settling into the seat felt like coming home. Even though DJ would rather ride English, her specialty, Patches' owners had requested Western training, at least for now. So Western it was.

She started the neck-reining review, turning him first in circles to the right and then the left, followed by figure eights. Patches let his displeasure at the slow pace be known as they moved from a walk to a jog. Instead of an easy-on-the-rider jog, he wanted to keep up a bone-jarring trot.

"Easy, fella." DJ repeatedly pulled him down. "Until you can manage this, you can't go any faster." When he refused to follow the figure-eight pattern, she brought him to a stop. He wasn't happy with that either, and he showed it by jigging to the side.

"You know, your manners leave a lot to be desired." The gelding tossed his head, jangling the bit, and stomped his front feet. DJ kept him in place. "I think tomorrow we'll put you on the hot walker so you can work some of this off before our training time." Patches snorted and sighed, as if giving up.

"Good fella." This time he went through his paces without a scolding.

"You are very good with him, DJ." Bridget had stopped to watch without DJ noticing. "I agree, putting a beginning rider up on him could cause some real problems."

"Whoever green-broke him let him get away with murder." DJ brought the horse to a stop in front of Bridget, who was leaning on the aluminum rail.

"He likes to run, that's for sure." Bridget reached out and stroked the gelding's nose. "But he will catch a judge's eye in the ring."

DJ leaned forward and stroked the now-sweaty neck. "That's what I told him. Okay, fella, back at it. Ready for a lope? A nice, easy rocking-chair lope?"

"Good luck." Bridget pushed away from the fence.

Half an hour later, Patches still fought the restrictions. He did *not* want to lope, he wanted to run. DJ dismounted and led him over to the barn, where she reached for a lead shank to snap onto his halter.

"Here, I'll hold him." James took the reins.

"Hey, James, thanks. You see what a pill he is?" DJ entered the tack room and returned with a running martingale. She undid the cinch and slipped the loop over it, settling the leather between Patches' front legs. Then she slipped the reins through the rings and checked to make sure all the adjustments were correct.

"That should help you with him." James stroked the horse's shoulder and helped adjust the leather straps.

"At least he won't be able to toss his head around." DJ patted the gelding's nose. "Sorry, fella, but you asked for it."

"I'll get the gate." James started across the dusty parking area.

"If I didn't know better, I'd say someone new is living in that boy's body." DJ swung aboard while muttering to no one in particular.

"You got it." Hilary led her mount into the sunlight. "You sure did work a miracle with that kid."

"Me?" DJ stopped herself from signaling Patches to move forward. She snapped her jaw closed.

"Well, he was buggin' you the worst, and then you worked at becoming his friend."

"I did?" DJ looked at Hilary as if maybe she'd gotten straw on the brain or something.

"Just a shame he's leaving."

"I know. I wish he weren't. Well, at least he'll be here for the Labor Day show." DJ thought about Hilary's comments while she rode across the parking lot and into the arena.

"Thanks for helping me, James. You gonna work Gray Bar now?"

"Yeah. After I finish my stalls. You got time to coach me on the V-bend for the trail class? She really hates that."

DJ swallowed a boulder of shock. James was asking for help. Wait till she told Gran! And here she'd laughed and groaned at Gran's suggestion to pray for James. Patches stopped flat in his journey around the ring. He didn't like the martingale.

DJ kept him at a jog, legs firm and whip in hand. Finally, after three circuits, the horse settled down and let out a sigh of defeat. Immediately, DJ nudged him into a lope. At first he tried bolting into a gallop, but the firm hand on his reins wouldn't allow that. And he couldn't get his head up. Sweat popped out on his neck, staining the smooth hide nearly black.

When he finally made two circuits of the arena at a gentle lope, DJ eased him back to a jog, then down to a walk. "Good boy. You might be stubborn, but you'll make it." She walked him around a few more times to help cool him down, then stopped to watch James work the parallel bars laid in a V formation in the center of the ring.

"Don't let her get so excited," DJ called out. "Make her stand in one place until she calms down. When you tense up, she gets tense."

James nodded.

DJ could see him unclench his jaw and his hands on the reins. When he settled down, so did Gray Bar.

"Good. Stay relaxed. Now, easy with your aids on

both hands and legs. Use small motions, but be consistent. You can do it."

James backed Gray Bar into the first side of the V. When they reached the point, they stopped.

"Good. Pat her. Tell her she's wonderful. You're doing fine."

With his left leg pressing against her side and the reins signaling to reverse, Gray Bar swung her rump around the sharp turn and continued backing out the opposite leg of the obstacle. When they stood free, James threw his arms around his horse's neck.

"We did it! Didn't tick one pole. First time ever."

DJ felt elation bubbling up. To see James so happy made her want to leap and dance. "I told you you could do it." Her bounce in the saddle made Patches sidestep. "Sorry, guy. Okay, James, now you and Gray Bar know what it feels like. Do it again, exactly the same." When James settled at the beginning again, DJ leaned forward, hands on her pommel. "You watch this, Patches, 'cause you're going to be doing the same thing pretty soon."

When DJ finally left for home, afternoon traffic was already increasing the car count on Reliez Valley Road. The sun beat down, hot and dry. For a change, the only breeze was created by her moving bike.

"Hey, DJ."

DJ hit the brakes. Amy waved and called from her bedroom window. DJ stopped at the bottom of the upward-sloped drive. "You finally better?"

"I'll be right down."

A moment later, with black hair flying, Amy leaped down the concrete steps and across the lawn.

"Yuk, you look awful." DJ sat with her feet on the ground, holding the bike upright, still on the street.

Technically, she wasn't at Amy's house. It wasn't as though DJ had called to her. "When you coming back to work?"

"Probably tomorrow. I'm all scabbed over now—"

"You can say that again." DJ could feel her own smooth skin crawl at the sight of the scabs all over Amy's face and neck. "You had a bad case, didn't you? You gonna have scars?"

"I hope not. I didn't scratch any on my face. Mom gave me gloves to wear at night, and I'm putting Vitamin E on 'em to help stop the scarring. Chicken pox is the pits."

"Yeah, and you never even have any zits." DJ fingered the prize she'd discovered on her chin that morning. "Think you can do the pony show tomorrow?"

Amy shook her head. "Sure, and scare all the kiddies away. I asked John. He said he'd go with you. But we owe him big time—and you know what that means."

"Ugh, paper route some morning when it's still dark."

"You got it." Amy shook her head. "But I didn't know what else to do." She lifted her shirt to show her midriff. "How about this for gross?" Spots covered her tanned skin.

"Pretty bad." DJ put one foot back on a pedal. "I better get going. If I don't get something to drink, I'll faint."

"And I need to get out of the sun. See ya in the morning." Amy spun away and headed for the house. Her little sister, Becky, waved from the doorway.

DJ waved back and pedaled the block to her house. She laid her bike by the garage and unlocked the front door. The empty smell struck her in the face. Not even the refrigerator hummed in the stillness. She sighed, dumped her backpack on the counter, and went out to the garage to put her bike away. There would be nothing out of place tonight to make her mom mad again. They were going out for dinner—and not for fast food, either.

After chugging a glass of water, she nosed in the refrigerator and pulled out stuff for sandwiches. Dumping it all on the counter, she crossed the room to check the answering machine for messages.

"Sorry, DJ, but an unexpected appointment came up, and I have to meet with the client tonight. Not sure what time I'll be home, but it'll probably be late. Let's plan on dinner out tomorrow night." DJ stabbed the erase button.

If only she could erase the hurt as easily.

3

WASN'T GRAN *EVER* COMING HOME?

That night, DJ pretended she was asleep when her mother knocked on the bedroom door. She heard the knob turn and the door open, but she lay on her side under the covers as if zonked to the world. *Serves her right*, she thought when she heard her mother sigh. The door closed with a soft click.

In the morning another note lay on the counter. After reading it, DJ crumbled it up and threw it in the trash. Tonight *she* didn't have time to go for dinner. And maybe she'd never have time again.

"You look like you lost your best friend, and I'm right here. What's up?" Amy leaped on her bike to join DJ in the pedal up the hill.

"Nothing." Eating worms was sounding like a possibility. *Fat worms, skinny worms, guess I'll go eat worms.* The song ran through her head.

"Hey, you don't have to bite my head off. I just got out of prison myself."

"You look funny with that hat on."

"Pardon me for living. My mother said that if I wanted to work, I had to wear this straw number out in

29

the sun. My Stetson doesn't have a wide enough brim."
Amy shook her head so the floppy straw brim did what
it did best—it flopped, then flew up in the wind.

"You'll scare the horses." DJ could feel her good humor coming back. She crested the hill and stopped at
the stop sign. "I'm glad you're here."

Amy puffed to a halt beside her. "So why play the
grouch?"

"My mother couldn't be bothered to come home in
time to take her daughter out to dinner last night like
she'd promised, that's all." DJ pushed off again. "No big
deal."

The wind felt good on her face when she coasted
down the hill to turn into the Academy drive. And now
that she'd dumped her gripe on Amy, she could even
smile up at a big crow scolding them from a Eucalyptus
tree. How come she could be so up one minute and
down in the pits the next? Maybe it was PMS. Lindy always blamed half her bad moods on it. DJ coasted to a
stop and leaned her bike against the barn in its usual
place. Another question to ask Gran—if and when she
ever came home.

DJ hurried through her chores at the Academy. Fast
brushing and slinging dirty shavings in record time was
becoming a habit. She couldn't work Patches until after
her class of beginners. "Okay, let's hustle." DJ went down
the line, hurrying her girls along.

"DJ, when we going up in Briones again?" Angie, a
chronic asthma sufferer, stopped brushing her horse to
ask.

"I cleared Friday with Bridget. We'll head out right
after our regular class. I told everyone last week."

"I wasn't here."

"Oh, I'm sorry. I should have called." DJ turned to the girl's pregnant mother standing off to the side. "Can Angie come?"

"That'll be fine. Then she can wash her horse in the afternoon to be ready for the show." Angie's mother laid a hand on her big belly. "This baby's due anytime, so we're just going day by day. My neighbor says she'll bring this daughter of mine down to ride if I'm in the hospital."

"Great. Okay, kids, let's get to work." DJ trotted ahead of them to slide the gate open. "Walk to the right please."

All three students grinned at her as they rode into the arena and did as she asked.

"Okay, backs straight but relaxed. Come on, Krissie, keep those reins even. Neck rein to the left—good. Now back to the right." The class proceeded as usual, only this time they were gearing up for a show. DJ treated them just as a judge would, ordering a walk, jog, back to a walk, lope, and reverse and repeat. When they were finished, they lined up in the middle. She walked down the line, inspecting the horses and riders, trying to keep a straight face.

She had them practice picking up their ribbons and leaving the arena. At the end of the hour, she motioned them into the shade of the roof. "You did good. I'm really proud of you. Angie, you gotta keep him on his toes. He'll go to sleep on you if you let him. Sam, remember, when you come up too close on another horse, turn a circle into the ring and come around again so you have plenty of room. Now, all of you, those saddles and bridles need to be so clean they shine. Angie, your horse is due for new shoes."

"Again?" Angie leaned on her saddle horn. "There goes my birthday money."

"The farrier will be here tomorrow. You want me to put your name on the list?"

"I guess." Her sigh could be heard clear into San Francisco.

"Okay, let's get 'em put away. Remember to bring your lunches with you on Friday, packed in saddlebags if you have them, and in smash-proof containers."

"We know."

"Just reminding you. And, Angie, make sure you bring your beesting kit." DJ held the gate open and let them file out. Their mothers were already waiting.

Training Patches took up the rest of the morning. She had to fly home to get ready for the pony party. It wouldn't do to go in her grungy clothes. And besides, she needed a shower. Even she could tell the BO wasn't coming from the horses.

When she and Amy's older brother, John, trotted up the street to one of the monstrous new houses at the top of hill on the west side of Reliez Valley Road, they were nearly late. The subdivision was so new, all the trees in the yards still looked like sticks. But the sodded lawns were green and kids played in the street. Some of them even ran after the pony until DJ told them to stop.

Balloons bobbed above the mailbox at the birthday house.

"Oh, I was beginning to worry you weren't coming," the young mother said when she answered the door. "Do you think you could bring the pony into the backyard? We have more room there."

"Sure. You have a side gate?" An image of Bandit

traipsing through the garage or the house flitted through DJ's mind.

"Oh, of course, I'm sorry."

DJ could tell the woman was flustered. If she was high-strung, what would the kids be like?

Like crazy is what they were. When one little boy bit him, John glared at DJ.

"Just help him down," DJ muttered under her breath. A little girl tugged at DJ's shirt.

"I wanna ride the pony." The whine would have cut logs.

"You'll get a turn in a minute."

"I wanna ride *now!*" The whine turned to a shriek.

The hostess came running over. "Is she hurt? What's the matter, dearest?"

"She's not taking turns too well." DJ kept the smile on her face in spite of her clenched teeth. If she had her way, the brat would never ride Bandit.

"Did you get that last picture?"

John glared at her. "Of course." He had red Kool-Aid stains on the front of his white T-shirt, thanks to a little boy who had refused to give up his drink. How come the mothers seemed to ignore the entertainment, sitting under a tree and visiting as if their kids belonged to someone else?

"Are *all* the parties like this?" John muttered through clenched teeth.

DJ shook her head, fighting to keep a smile on her face.

"Ow-w-ie! He bit me!" The ear-shattering scream from the vicinity of her left knee made DJ's heart jump. She looked down. A tow-headed boy was running in place and screaming in megadecibels that increased in direct proportion to the speed of his feet. DJ wished she could clap her hands over her ears, but she had to see what was wrong.

Bandit pulled back on the reins, a clump of grass dangling from the side of his mouth. His eyes rolled white, and his ears smashed flat against his head.

DJ didn't know which to work with—the boy or the pony.

"He bit me!" The kid clutched one hand with the other.

The hostess ran out of the house. Another woman came to help her. Both pestered the howling boy with a thousand questions, all the while glaring at DJ, John, and poor Bandit.

DJ couldn't see any blood. Since the others were there to care for the child, she opted to attend to Bandit. John lifted the current rider down from the saddle and set her on the ground. Her face screwed up, ready to wail, in sympathy for the screamer.

It took all of DJ's will to keep calm. "He gave Bandit some grass and his finger got in the way." Her tone sang comfort to the horse while her words filled John in on what had happened.

"You shouldn't bring a horse that bites to a children's party." One of the women now held the sniffling child on her hip.

"I told them not to feed the pony." Again DJ kept her voice calm. Inside, she wanted to scream. *It's not Bandit's fault. It's your fault! Keep a watch on your bratty kid*. This was the boy who had dumped his drink on John's shirt. A real charmer if ever there was one. At that moment, DJ was glad she'd never had younger brothers and sisters—what if they'd turned out like these kids?

She rubbed Bandit's ears and waited for things to calm down.

"Bad pony." The boy scrubbed his cheeks with grubby hands and kicked his mother to let him down.

DJ caught a look from John that made her bite her lip.

"Who's next for a pony ride?" She pointed to a little girl in jeans and a sideways Giants baseball cap. "You haven't ridden yet. How about if we swap our Western hat for yours while you ride?"

"No." The little girl clutched her hat.

John started to say something, but instead just lifted the child into the saddle. "You won't have a Western picture like everyone else," he warned her.

"I don't care. Giddy-up." She slapped her legs against the saddle.

DJ led her off around the yard. This kid was a corker. But from the look on her face, she loved to ride. She leaned forward and stroked Bandit's neck, not bothering to hang on to the saddle horn like the others. "Good pony. What's his name?"

"Bandit."

"Nice Bandit. I'm gonna have a pony someday."

DJ nodded. "I hope you do." Now this was a neat kid. Not a brat—she just knew what she wanted. DJ gave her an extra turn around the yard.

"Okay, that's all for today." DJ checked to make sure all the children had had their turns.

John opened the back of the camera and handed the pictures to the hostess. She gave him an envelope and a frosty "thank you."

DJ made sure they had all their gear and led Bandit

toward the gate. Once out on the street, John checked the envelope.

"Just wanted to make sure she paid us. What a pain!"

"That has to be the worst party we've had, worse even than the one where the kids tracked horse manure onto the woman's brand-new white carpet. That's why we bring the pooper scooper now." Just then Bandit lifted his tail and plopped some green offerings onto the asphalt.

John glared at DJ. She held the reins while he untied the metal scooper and did his chore, dumping the manure under a bush when they came to one. "Just don't ask me to help with these parties again—ever." His words matched the narrow line of his mouth clenched over clamped teeth.

"They could at least have offered us something to drink."

By the time DJ and John told Amy all about the pony party, she lay on the floor kicking her heels and hooting.

"John, it's never been *that* bad. You guys are making this up, right?"

John glared at her and nudged her with his toe.

"Hee-hee, I love it." Amy sat upright and clasped her arms around her bent knees. "Bandit bit him." This time her giggles infected DJ much like a germ, and when she described the bratty boy dumping his drink down John's shirt, she too collapsed against the back of the sofa.

"Th-thanks for he-helping." She glanced at the scowl on John's face and grabbed her middle. This was the kind of laughter that couldn't be stopped. Every time she and Amy looked at each other or John, they laughed till they hiccuped. "I'm going to wet my pants if we don't q-q-quit."

John fought to keep the frown on his face. He gave it his best effort. But the grin broke through. It started with a snort. Then a hoot. He leaped to his feet. "You two can waste your time carrying on like this, but I have better things to do."

"B-b-better th-things to . . ." The two were off again. DJ made a fast charge down the hall. It's hard to run with your legs crossed.

When she came out of the bathroom, Mrs. Yamamoto had brought homemade lemonade and cookies into the family room. "Here, you giggling gerties, you need something to cool you off. John, I hear you really earned your money today." Her smile set DJ and Amy off again. John took his glass and a handful of cookies and left the room.

"You two better never ask me to help again," he called back. "You're totally nuts to do those parties." He stomped up the stairs to his room.

"You two." Mrs. Yamamoto shook her head when she left the room.

DJ could hear the younger kids playing outside on the swing set. She looked at her watch. She should get home. She wasn't supposed to be here anyway—but she just *had* to tell Amy about the party.

"See ya tomorrow." She headed for the door. "You remember we're taking my beginning class up to Briones on Friday?"

"Yep. Mom said I could go." Amy followed DJ all the way to the sidewalk. "When do you get off restriction?"

"Just in time for school. Big deal, huh?" DJ swung her leg over her bike. "I never thought being grounded could be so bad." She shook her head. "Sure wish you could come home with me. I hate it there all by myself."

Another message on the machine didn't do anything to improve the evening. Her mother couldn't make it again.

DJ tried to shrug it off. Who cared anyway? She didn't.

But if she didn't care, why didn't drawing a new horse sketch make her feel better? One fingernail started to bleed, she'd chewed it down so far. Good thing she didn't say the word she thought. That kind of language wasn't allowed in their house. Even an empty one.

4

I WONDER WHAT MY FATHER WAS LIKE? DJ lay on her bed, one leg crossed over her raised knee. She swung the upper foot in time with the rhythm of her snapping gum. Snapping gum was another one of those habits that made her mother see red. There were sure a lot of things that set Mom off, especially lately.

DJ started listing them. Her bike left out—anything left out. She could hear her mother's demand. "A place for everything, and everything in its place." She hated that line. On with her list: horse-scented clothes, whether on her daughter or left in the hamper; loud music; mouthing off; any clothes DJ liked; two-fingered whistles in the house ... DJ sighed. Face it. Nearly everything she did set her mother off now that Gran wasn't around.

But that was enough thinking about her mother. *So, what about my father? What do I really know about my dad?* She wrinkled her forehead, trying to remember anything her mother or Gran had said about him. One thing they'd both said was that she got her love of horses from him. And she must look like him because she sure didn't look like any of her mother's relatives. There had to be some reason no one talked about him. Was he in jail for murder or something? Her mother must have really liked him at one time. After all, babies didn't just come out of the sky.

Her mind followed this new thought. What would it feel like to really be in love with someone? Some girls at school thought they were in love, and they talked about guys all the time. DJ's leg bounced more quickly. In love—fiddle! She'd never even kissed a boy, not really. You couldn't count Raymond's peck on her cheek. But if she'd wanted to, he probably would have—kissed her on the mouth that is.

But you had to feel something pretty special to let someone slobber all over you like actors did in the movies. DJ cracked her gum. "I'd rather have horse slobber any day."

Someday there *would* be someone special in her life. Gran said God had one person in mind for her; she'd been praying for him since DJ was a little girl. And if love was like the glow surrounding Gran and Joe, it couldn't be too bad. Kind of fantastic actually. DJ turned over and wrapped her arms around her pillow. Not having Gran around was a bummer.

Not having *anyone* around was worse than a bummer. Only four more days till she was off restrictions. She was counting the minutes. DJ made sure everything was put away, the laundry done, and the family room picked up—not that it needed much—before she went to bed. She wasn't taking any chances on getting her grounding extended.

Her mother knocked on the door and said good-night when she came home. It made DJ miss Gran even more.

Friday morning DJ packed her lunch for the picnic,

putting a sandwich in a sturdy plastic container just as she'd told the girls to do. She stood at the open fridge door; they were out of fruit. No chips, either. She should have ridden her bike to the store last night. At least there were cookies. She dug a carrot out of the drawer and peeled it. Some lunch. Maybe Amy would grab an apple or something for her.

"Thanks, bud," she yelled over her shoulder when Amy returned from getting a nectarine for DJ.

"You're welcome. Are all three going today?"

"Yep. Unless Mrs. Lincoln had her baby during the night."

The early morning felt crisp, and a breeze blew that made DJ glad she'd put a sweatshirt over her T-shirt. She could see trails of clouds peeping over the hills to the west. When San Francisco Bay was foggy, mornings here by Briones were cool. And wonderful. She sniffed the air, breathing deep in spite of the hill they were pedaling up.

At the Academy she and Amy rushed through their chores. Amy picked up some of DJ's stalls so she'd have time to train Patches. Once in the ring, the gelding jigged sideways, tossing his head and generally being a number one pain.

"You sure are a stubborn one." DJ leaned forward and patted his neck. "Keep testing me every day, hoping I'll get soft?" Patches flicked his ears back and forth, taking in all the sights and sounds. With a sigh, he settled into an even jog, following her reining instructions without a hitch.

Half an hour later, he stopped immediately when DJ barely tightened the reins. "Well, I'll be." She shook her head. "If you behaved like this every day, I'd say you were ready for your owners. You could enter a walk/jog class and come out with a blue." The thought burst like Fourth-of-July sparklers. No, it was too late. The Labor Day show was next week, and she hadn't cleared it with the owners. But Patches sure would look good out there. And they'd find out how he did under pressure.

"You're one smart fella." She dismounted and led him out the gate. "Thanks, Ames," she said when they entered the barn. Patches' stall was cleaned and new shavings spread. "When are you going to have time to work with Josh?"

"This afternoon after the ride. If he doesn't know the routine by now, he never will." Amy leaned on her shovel handle. She started to scratch a spot on her face and instead used the tail of her T-shirt to wipe the sweat away.

"You look lots better."

"Better'n what? At least it only looks like a bad case of the zits now. Sure makes me feel sorry for anyone who has bad skin. I never appreciated mine before." She dabbed her forehead again.

DJ finished putting her gear away and trotted Patches out to the hot walker. She unsnapped Megs and brought her back into the barn.

Two of her students giggled their way to the barn, saddles over their arms. Their mothers brought up the rear with saddlebags and helmets.

"We'll be back about two, right?" Sam asked.

"Angie and Sam need to wash their horses. We did mine last night." Krissie hung her saddle over the door. "And I soaped this thing 'til my arm almost fell off."

DJ tapped her on top of the head. "Good for you. That arm looks pretty well attached to me."

Krissie giggled. "You know what I mean."

Angie and her mother arrived next. Mrs. Lincoln handed DJ the beesting kit. "I'd rather this was in your saddlebag than hers. You be careful now, dear." She gave her daughter a hug.

Angie rolled her eyes. "Yeah, Mom. See you about five?"

DJ smiled and turned to her crew as soon as the last of the mothers walked away. "Okay, kids, let's hit the arena. Last class before the big show, so let's do it right."

"And only three more classes before school. Yuk." Sam shook her head and made a face. "I hate school, just hate it!"

"I'd rather ride every day like DJ."

"You think I don't go to school?" DJ tugged on Angie's ponytail. "Dream on. Come on, strap on your helmets. You're sure poking along today." She went from horse to horse, checking to make sure each saddle was positioned over the withers and the girths smooth.

"We know how to saddle up by now." Sam stood back so DJ could check.

"I know you do, but double-checking is my job. You wouldn't want your horse to get a saddle sore, would you?"

"No." Sam stroked her horse's nose.

DJ picked up a front foot. "You didn't pick this enough. See the manure caked here by the frog?"

Sam nodded. "It was too dark in there to see good." DJ turned and gave her young pupil *the* look. She'd copied it from Bridget, who was a master at it.

"Don't look at me like that." Sam tied her horse and dug a pick out of her bucket. "You'd think . . ." She looked up at DJ and swallowed whatever else she'd been going to say. Her lower lip stuck out until she bit down on it. She checked each hoof before dumping the pick back into the bucket and leading her horse out to the arena.

"Ya did good." DJ walked beside her. She knew what was going through Sam's head. One time Bridget had caught her trying to rush. She'd never dared to do it again.

By the time the class was finished, the sun had baked any coolness out of the air. The girls got drinks at the fountain beside the barn, slung their saddlebags up behind their Western saddles, and tied them down with latigos.

DJ let them through the gate that led to the trails, Amy going first. Megs, saddled English for DJ, seemed glad to have a rider. She pricked her ears and picked up her feet to catch up. "Easy, girl. They won't get away from us."

Raising in her stirrups, DJ stretched her legs and hugged her shoulders up to her ears. If—she quickly corrected herself—*when* she had a horse of her own, she'd ride up here every week. Maybe when Joe got his cutting horse, they could ride together. Would Major like trail-riding?

Once inside the park, the shade up the trail felt like a cool blanket. DJ looked up to see a squirrel jump from one tree branch across the trail to another tree. He scolded them as though they'd invaded his kingdom.

"There's another squirrel." Angie, who rode in front of DJ, pointed to a particularly fat squirrel, the sunlight through the branches glinting off his red fur. He dropped bits from the pinecone he rotated in his paws, stuffing its nuts into already fat cheeks.

DJ and Angie let the others get ahead so they could

keep watching the squirrel's antics. He dropped the core of the cone and, flicking his tail, ran back up the branch and around the tree trunk.

"We had a squirrel nest in a tree in our backyard. Three babies. The mother yelled at us if we got too close." Angie nudged her horse forward. "They're all grown now. They come down to our deck for peanuts."

"My grandpa used to tame squirrels, but we haven't had any in our yard for a while. The neighbors cut down their tree and the squirrels left." The two girls rode side by side. "You excited about the show tomorrow?"

"Scared. When I get too scared I throw up. What if I throw up tomorrow?" Angie shuddered. "I'll just die. I know I will."

They crested the top of the last hill and rode into the open meadow. Briones Crest Trail stalked the higher ridge off to their left. The green grass of spring had dried to straw, painting the hills in shades of tan and gold. Two black turkey vultures rode the thermals above them, seeming to drift without a flicker of feather.

"We riding to the top?" Amy called back. She and the other riders were trotting the fire road that curved around the meadow and up to the trail.

"'Course. We can eat when we come back down." DJ nudged Megs into a canter. "Come on, Angie, let's catch 'em."

By the time they'd ridden to the top of the crest trail, where they watched a red fox slinking over the top of yet another hill, they were more than ready to eat.

"Wait a minute." DJ hissed the command. "Stop."

When all were silent, she pointed to a gentle hollow in a hill across the small valley. Three deer grazed as if they'd never before seen humans. One raised its head, big ears poised to catch any unusual sound. "Ohhh," Angie breathed a sigh of delight. "They are so pretty."

"The little one must be this year's fawn," Amy spoke softly, moving only her lips.

One of the horses tossed its head, the bit jangling loudly in the silence.

The other two deer raised their heads. With a single motion, they leaped the dirt bank and bounded up the hill. Once they disappeared over the crest, DJ nudged Megs forward.

"Come on, let's go eat."

They dismounted under some trees and, after removing their bridles, slipped on halters and tied their horses to low branches. While two girls used a fallen log for a chair, the rest sat cross-legged in the dead leaves and forest duff.

"Did you check for poison oak?" DJ finished inspecting everyone's tie knots before joining them with the lunch out of her saddlebag.

"Yep, Amy did." Angie leaned back against the log. She took a long drink from her water flask. "I could eat a bear."

"Yuk."

"Better'n eating a horse."

"Angie!" The other girls groaned in unison.

For a time there was only the sound of munching. DJ crunched a carrot stick between bites of her sandwich. She and Amy swapped grins. This was about as good as it got.

"Just think, when you have Major next summer, maybe we can both go on the Sierra trip." Amy leaned back on her elbows. "I think that would be the best thing ever."

"How old do you have to be?" Sam looked up from digging for something in her saddlebag.

"Twelve, unless you have parents who can ride along." DJ swatted at a yellow jacket that was exploring the top of her soda can. "Get out of here, bee."

Angie ducked when it flew by her. "I wish my dad could take me. He says he loves to ride but just doesn't have time."

"Mine too." Krissie put the lid back on her sandwich container. "Just think, riding every day for a whole week!"

"Camping out . . . cooking over a fire."

"Ants in your food." Amy brushed one of the tiny creatures off her hand. "They show up everywhere." She ducked and shooshed the persistent yellow jacket away. "Beat it, buzzer."

"Owww. Oh no!" Angie swatted at her hand.

"Did he sting you?" DJ felt her heart leap.

"Yes. DJ, help." Angie scrambled to her feet. Eyes wide, her mouth an O. "Help me. I won't be able to breathe!"

5

DJ LEAPED TO HER FEET. She dashed toward the horses, only slowing in time to keep them from shying. Why hadn't she brought the saddlebags with her? Or at least the bee kit. What kind of a teacher was she?

She fumbled in the first saddlebag but came up empty-handed. She could hear Amy cautioning the girls to be calm. *Please, God, don't let Angie quit breathing.* The prayer beat in DJ's mind at the same pace as her thudding heart.

Megs backed away when DJ hurried around her to get into the other saddlebag. "Easy, girl." But DJ could tell her own actions were anything but easy. *Calm down!* She made herself stop and take a deep breath as her fingers closed over the plastic box. But her mind continued to race. *I've never given a person a shot before. What do I do?* A more calm voice spoke gently but firmly. *Just read the instructions. You've seen lots of shots given, just do the same.*

"She's starting to wheeze," Samantha called. "Hurry, DJ."

"It's going to be all right, Angie, take it easy. The more

uptight you get, the worse it will be." Amy acted as if they did this every day.

What if the shot doesn't work? The reassuring voice came again. *It will.* Was this what listening to God's voice was like? DJ felt herself calming down. She took another deep breath as she dropped to her knees on the ground beside the wheezing girl.

Angie's chest rose and fell with each struggling breath, as though she were being pumped by a bellows—slowly. Sweat broke out on her forehead.

Angie looked up at DJ. "I don't want to die."

"You won't." Amy wiped the girl's hair back from her forehead. "Come on, you've been through this before. You can tell DJ what to do."

"No, I don't remember." Her breathing sounded like a marathon runner's who'd just crossed the finish line.

In, out, in, out. DJ could feel her own breaths come in time with Angie's, as though she were trying to breathe for the girl.

DJ held the prefilled syringe between her teeth and ripped open the square packet of alcohol rub. She took the syringe out of her mouth. "Easy, Angie—just bend your arm like you do at the doctor's office. Good. Now we'll wipe it . . ." DJ's actions followed her words. She dropped the gauze square on the ground. "And . . ." She closed her eyes. *Please, God.* With a quick jerk, she pulled the cap off and, without giving herself time to think, stabbed the needle into Angie's bicep.

After depressing the plunger, DJ pulled the needle out and sat back on her heels. Her heart raced like a bike going downhill with a tailwind. She put the cap back on the syringe. "Thank you, God." Her whisper blended with the agonized sound of Angie's breathing.

"That . . . didn't even . . . hurt. You're good." Angie leaned back against Amy's knees and chest. Her eyes closed and she tried to take a deep breath. Instead, she coughed.

"Easy, just think about how much fun we've had. Seeing the deer on the hillside." DJ kept her voice smooth and gentle. The singsong worked with horses, why not a sick kid?

"You want me to ride down and get help?" Amy asked, her hands busy smoothing Angie's forehead.

DJ forced her careening mind to stop and think. "Maybe you better. But Mrs. Lincoln said this stuff really works, if we get it into Angie fast enough."

"Do you think we did—get it in quick enough, I mean?"

"I'll go," Sam volunteered.

DJ looked up to see the scared expressions on the faces of the other girls. "No, Sam, but thanks. Amy will get help, if anyone. I can't take a chance on someone else getting hurt." *Why'd I ever let this happen? Maybe Angie shouldn't do this kind of thing. But she wants to so bad. Why couldn't the stupid bee have stung me instead?*

"I'm getting better, DJ. I can feel it." Angie reached out a shaky hand and stuck it in DJ's.

A rash of relieved giggles broke out from the other girls. Both flopped back on the ground as if someone had just cut their puppets' strings. "Angie, that was the scariest thing I ever saw."

"Man, DJ, you did that just like a nurse." Krissie pointed a finger at DJ. "You are awesome."

Angie sat up on her own. While she was still wheezing, now it was more like a whistle than a freight train. "Thanks, DJ, you saved my life."

DJ blinked her eyes and gritted her teeth. She would not cry now, not in front of these girls. She looked up at Amy to see a sheen of moisture in her dark eyes. A smile trembled at the sides of her mouth.

DJ rolled her lips together, licked them, and took a deep breath. "Well, girls, you all finished with your lunches?" She looked around at heads shaking no. "Okay, then let's do that. If I don't get something to drink, I might faint."

Amy handed DJ her water bottle. "Drink fast. We don't want any fainting up here. We might have to give you a shot . . ."

"A shot of water will do just fine." DJ glugged and felt the boulder stuck in her throat go down with the water.

Krissie picked up the syringe and the leftover pieces of the bee kit. "Here, DJ, we don't want to be litterbugs."

"No way." Sam started to giggle, then Krissie. DJ and Amy tried to keep straight faces. Angie giggled, wheezed, and giggled some more. "We c-could litter th-the ground with b-bees." She fell back against the log, her laughter growing stronger with each easing breath.

"Dead bees."

"Definitely dead bees." They all rolled on the ground, clutching their stomachs and wiping their eyes.

"Wh-what's s-so funny?" DJ made the mistake of looking at Amy. She knew better.

"G-got me."

Finally the giggles let up.

"I have to go to the bathroom." Angie lay on the ground, the back of one hand over her eyes.

"Pick a tree—any tree." Sam waved her hand. "We have plenty."

"Sure, and get stung on my rear this time."

That did it. The girls fell against one another, their giggles floating up through the branches like a strange kind of bird song. DJ tried to take another drink from the water bottle and ended up blowing the water out her nose.

"Ow. Knock it off. See what you made me do?"

By now Angie could laugh without wheezing. She was making up for lost time. Every time one person calmed down, another started in. Finally they all lay flat on the leaves and dried grass. *Better giggling than crying*, DJ thought, gazing up through the gnarly oak branches above them. Sunbeams outlined the leaves. DJ drew in a deep breath and let a prayer float up toward heaven. *Thank you, God. I couldn't have done it without you.*

"DJ, you want one of my cookies?" Angie nudged DJ's shoulder with her boot toe.

"Sure." DJ pushed herself upright and accepted the offer. Munching and sitting spraddle-legged, she studied her group. While they all had bits of leaves and twigs in their hair and could use a good dusting, no one looked the worse for wear. Her heart had resumed residence in its normal place, and when she held up a hand, it no longer trembled like a leaf in windstorm.

"Thanks, Angie. Good cookie."

"I made them."

"Wow, you can come bake cookies for me anytime." DJ rose to her feet and dusted off her rear. "You guys ready to hit the trail?"

"No, I'd rather stay up here." Angie finished packing her saddlebags.

"Yeah, well, if one of those mean bees comes after you again, we're fresh outta bee kit." DJ extended a hand to pull the girl to her feet. "And I'm just so grateful you're all right that next time I'll pack a whole case of 'em." She turned Angie around and brushed her off. The girls took turns doing the same for one another. By the time they rode back into the academy lot, the beesting was nearly a forgotten incident, until the girls started telling their mothers about it.

"Should we call your mother and have her take you to the doctor?" DJ stopped by Angie's stall where she was unsaddling her horse.

Angie shook her head. "Once I'm breathing okay again, the doctor can't do anything. I'm just a little tired. Right now I need to wash my horse and soap my saddle. Mom'll be here about five. Don't worry about me, okay? I hate having people worry and watch me."

DJ nodded. "I'd feel the same. Holler if you need help."

She accepted the other mothers' thanks, reminded them of next week's schedule, and headed for Bridget's office.

"I hear you are the hero of the day." Bridget turned from the filing cabinet where she'd been inserting papers into their proper files.

"How'd you know?"

"A little bird. I am really proud of you; it sounds as though you handled yourself in a totally professional and competent manner."

"Bridget, I was so scared. More than I've been any time in my whole life."

"Heroes are not necessarily brave when the chips are down; they just keep on going, doing what needs to be done. You kept your head about you—"

"I prayed hard."

"That helps too. The main thing is, you did not panic.

I have always felt I could count on you, and now I know it." Bridget sat on the edge of her desk.

"You should have seen the giggle fit we had when it was over and Angie was starting to breath easy again."

"Natural reaction. To laugh, cry, get mad, giddy."

"*I* felt like crying. So did Amy."

"That would have been normal, like I said."

"But it might have scared the girls."

"Right. That is why I say you are a hero. You got the job done and thought of others first. You can always fall apart later, if need be."

DJ could feel her lower lip tremble. "I hate crying." She swallowed hard and rolled her eyes toward the ceiling. Blinking quickly, she fought back the tears.

"There is nothing wrong with crying. Tears help wash both the eyes and the soul."

"I gotta check on the girls." DJ bolted from the office.

Mrs. Lincoln had tears in her eyes when she told DJ thank you. She wrapped her arms around DJ and hugged her as though she'd invented hugging. And hugging with a baby-big stomach between them wasn't easy. DJ grinned.

"Hey, what was that?" DJ pulled back and stared down at the mound under Mrs. Lincoln's top.

"The baby said thank you, too." Mrs. Lincoln patted her tummy.

DJ's eyes traveled from the huge belly to the woman's face. "Did you feel it?"

"Of course. This one's been kicking like he plans to join a World Cup soccer team tomorrow."

"I never knew it felt like that."

Mrs. Lincoln took DJ's hand and laid it on her abdomen. The baby let loose with a one-two punch that bounced DJ's hand.

"Wow! Didja see that?"

Angie and her mother burst out laughing. "We see it all the time. If this one's as active after it's born as it is now, we'll be chasing him down the street in a couple of weeks."

DJ glanced up for permission and, at Mrs. Lincoln's nod, put her hand back on the woman's belly. When nothing happened, she looked up again.

"Guess we wore him out."

"You know for sure it's a boy?"

"No, so it's a good thing there are girls' soccer teams, too. You ready to leave, Angie? We have tons of things to do."

DJ watched them drive away, waving in return when Angie rolled down the minivan's window to wave good-bye. Babies had never seemed so real to her. And just breathing had never been something she thought to be grateful about. If only Gran were here. What stories DJ had to tell her!

When she walked into the empty house after pedaling home, the light was blinking on the answering machine. She pushed the rewind button.

After a squawk, the machine let loose with Gran's voice.

"Hi, darlin's. We've been having such a wonderful time, Joe and I decided to stay a bit longer."

DJ felt her chin drop to the floor. "No, you can't do that!"

6

"JUST TEASING! We'll be home Sunday night."

DJ sagged against the wall. "Not funny, Gran. Not funny at all."

The next message was from her mother. "If you get home before 4:30, call me. Otherwise we'll plan on going out for dinner; you choose the place."

"I'll believe that when I see it." DJ checked the clock. It was already 4:45. She looked down at her clothes. If her mother caught her looking and smelling like horse and the woodsy ground she'd lain on, they'd never go out.

She shucked her clothes by the washing machine and threw the shirt and jeans in, along with others in the hamper. Then while that started running, she charged upstairs to shower.

Where should we go? Pizza? Nah. She thought of places and discarded them as fast while the water pounded on her head and shoulders. By the time she wrapped a towel around her stringy wet blond hair, she'd decided on Chinese. If they ordered enough, they could warm it up for dinner tomorrow night. Only two more days and Gran would be home.

For a change, DJ and her mother spent an entire evening together without arguing. They each chose a dish at the restaurant and even tried a new one, Mongolian Beef, which they both loved. And when her mother suggested a movie and ice cream afterward, DJ nearly fainted.

"You . . . you don't have to study tonight?"

"Nope. And I didn't bring any work home either. We should mark this on the calendar." Lindy flipped the lock so DJ could get into the car. " 'Course I can always find more to do. . . .' "

"Who can't." DJ thought of the mess she'd left in her bedroom. She'd made sure the door was closed so her mother couldn't see in.

Later, at the ice cream parlor, Lindy licked hot fudge sauce off her spoon and bobbed it at DJ. "You know, about that emergency with Angie. I'm not sure I could have given a shot like that."

"There was nothing else to do. It wasn't much different from giving a horse an injection." DJ twirled her spoon in the fudge sauce. "Making sure to give her the right amount would have been worse. This syringe was all loaded."

"Still, it took plenty of nerve."

DJ watched her mother from under her eyelashes. What was going on? Could this be a peace offering? Lindy never ate ice cream—said there was too much fat in it—let alone a hot fudge sundae. And after popcorn at the movie and Chinese food?

"I think I'm going to burst." Lindy wiped her mouth with her napkin.

DJ could hear Gran's voice in her ear. *Your mother loves you, she just doesn't always know how to show it.*

*She's been so tied up at work and school, she let mother-
hood slip right past her.*

They didn't say much on the way home, but what was
new? They'd already talked more in one evening than a
typical month. And when her mother thanked her for a
nice time, DJ's red flags really went up. Danger! Warning! *What's going on?*

DJ left for the Academy in the morning before her
mother woke up.

"Get real," Amy shouted at DJ's back when they pedaled up the hill. "Maybe your mom just wants to spend
more time with you. You know, that old 'quality time'
thing. I think grown-ups get hung up on that pretty easily."

"But she didn't yell at me once. Wouldn't you be sus-
picious?"

"Nah, I'd be grateful."

After clipping Patches to the hot walker where he
could dance off some of his energy, Amy and DJ rushed
through their chores so they could take Patches and
Josh into the ring at the same time. DJ wanted Patches
to get used to having other horses around him when he
had a rider.

"All right, settle down, you hyper thing." DJ pulled
the gelding to a standstill for the third time. Even after
his hot walker workout and four times around the ring,
Patches wanted to race whoever else was present. Sweat
from his excitement already darkened his shoulders.
She watched Amy put Josh through his paces. The two
of them looked as though they were welded together.
"See, silly, that's what we're supposed to look like. We're
supposed to work together."

Patches jigged in place, his front feet raising puffs of

dust as they pounded the ground. When he finally relaxed, DJ loosened the reins and let him walk. "And here
I thought you were ready for your owners. You'd shake
them senseless." When Patches finally managed to make
an entire circuit of the ring at a walk, she let him jog.
He made it with only one return to a walk this time.

"Looks like he's trying." Amy rode beside her for a
circuit.

"Yeah, trying my patience."

"You know what I mean."

"Sure, he's trying to run. He wants to catch up to anyone ahead of him."

"Don't worry about it, DJ. Pretty soon you'll have him
obeying just like Diablo did. I know you will."

This time when DJ neck reined Patches in a circle so
he could go back the other way, he minded. "So there is
hope for you after all," she muttered.

They had to rush to get ready for their next pony
party, but it was worth it. The hostess stayed with them
the entire time, making sure all the kids took turns. She
brought DJ and Amy punch to drink and offered them
ice cream and cake if they'd stay longer and let the children ride again. When she offered to pay them an extra
ten dollars, the girls agreed.

"This sure beat the last one," DJ said when they trotted Bandit up the road toward the Academy. "Poor John.
He hated it. And those kids were just awful."

"We could tell John about this one and blame him for
the other." Amy wore a sly grin. This was her chance to
get even with a big brother who thought teasing his
younger sister was what he was put on this earth for.

But John wasn't home when they got there; he and
his dad had taken a load of yard clippings to the dump.

"Fiddle." DJ plopped down on the curb in front of the house.

"Double fiddle." Amy joined her. "Well, at least the party went well and we made extra money."

"We have only one party to go. You know, I've been thinking—"

"No." Amy shook her head so hard her black hair swished her cheeks. "We're not keeping on with the parties. Once school starts, we just don't have time."

"But . . ."

"No. Nada. Ixnay."

DJ wrinkled her mouth to one side. "Next summer?"

"Maybe. If we don't come up with a better idea by then. But if we do the pony parties, we are going to train Bandit to pull a cart."

"It's a deal." The two slapped high fives.

DJ entered her house to the sound of the vacuum cleaner and her mother's easy-listening music playing on the stereo. "I'm home." She heard the vacuum shut off.

Even for cleaning house, her mother managed to wear things that matched. The observation crossed DJ's mind at the same time as she registered the scowl her mother sported. A frown of that type caused wrinkles, but DJ didn't feel stupid or daring enough to comment.

"Have you noticed your room and bathroom lately?" The tone matched the face. They were certainly back to normal. The evening before must have been a fluke.

"I know. I was in a hurry."

"It doesn't take any more time to hang up the towel than to drop it on the floor."

The words pricked like a burr under a saddle. "I know, I'll take care of it." DJ bit her lip to keep from answering back and climbed the stairs to her room. Gran would say to count her blessings. Last night had been a blessing—a fun one. She sighed. If only it had lasted.

The next morning revealed another hole in DJ's life. She attended church with the Yamamotos since Gran was out of town. She'd thought of asking her mother to take her, but they hadn't said much to each other the night before. In fact, they hadn't said anything. The house didn't need an air conditioner with her mother in *that* kind of mood.

DJ looked up at the stained-glass shepherd behind the altar. Jesus looked so kind; He held the lamb as if He really cared. The window made DJ miss Gran even more. She needed a hug, a Gran-type hug. It wouldn't be long now until the newlyweds returned. During the moment for silent prayer, she prayed for a safe flight for Gran and Joe. But the pastor started talking again before she got around to praying for her mother.

Later, at home, DJ asked, "Who's picking Gran and Joe up at the airport?"

"Robert. He'll take them back to Joe's for his car, and then they'll come out here." Lindy looked up from the book she was reading. "I've told you this before."

"I forgot." DJ gnawed on the nub of her right thumbnail. "You don't think they had an accident or something?"

Lindy shook her head. "No. The flight was probably late, that's all. Or maybe there's traffic, or they had something else they had to do first." Her tone said she was losing patience.

DJ headed to the kitchen for a drink of water. "They're here!" She set the glass in the sink and barreled out the front door. "Gran! You're back!" She flew around the hood of the car and threw her arms around the petite woman just emerging from the front seat.

"Oh, my Darla Jean, if you've missed me as much as I've missed you . . ." Gran patted her granddaughter's back and hugged her again. Arm in arm they came around the car, talking nonstop.

"Hi, DJ." Joe leaned his arms on the top of the open car door. "Lindy." He raised a hand in greeting to the woman standing in the doorway.

"Hi." DJ caught herself. She'd almost forgotten about Joe. "Won't you come in?" There, she'd remembered her manners. She stood back to let Gran hug Lindy and Joe do the same. A funny kind of feeling invaded her stomach. Not a ha-ha kind of funny but an oh-oh kind. "You want me to get your suitcases, Gran?"

"No, we left them at Joe's. Come see the things we brought you."

The oh-oh turned to an oh no and left DJ with a new hole in her heart. Gran wouldn't be staying here. She wouldn't be sitting in her chair, Bible in her lap, to tell DJ goodbye in the morning. *She won't be here when I come home from the Academy.*

"Darla Jean, whatever is the matter?" Gran turned and wrapped an arm around DJ's waist. "You look as though you've seen a ghost."

"You're not going to stay here." DJ choked the words out.

"Of course not, but soon we'll move into our new house and we'll only be a mile away." She moved forward, drawing DJ with her. "You knew that, surely."

"Yeah, I just never thought about it." DJ didn't say what filled her heart and mind. *But, Gran, I need you here. Mom and I, we aren't doing so good. I need you.* She studied the raw spot on her thumb cuticle. Gran looked so happy. So did Joe. She couldn't be a brat again—she just couldn't. *Shape up! Don't ruin it for them again by saying something stupid. You want to be grounded for life?*

7

SMILING AND SAYING "thank you" when you want to cry isn't easy. But DJ did it. She pasted on a smile, laughed in the right places, and even said something nice to Joe. But inside . . . she was a mess. DJ didn't dare look directly at Gran. She was too good at reading eyes. And from the burning, DJ knew hers must be red. Or at the very least, sad and scared.

She held her new scooped-neck T-shirt up to her chest. Three dolphins leaped and dove across the turquoise fabric. "It's a beaut. And the shorts are perfect. Thanks." She admired the swirly skirt and tank top they'd brought her mother. And oohed and aahed at the pictures. Maybe she should try out for drama when she got to high school. This was turning into an Academy Award performance.

"Someday we'll go back and take you with us to snorkel." Gran handed DJ a picture taken under water that showed fish they usually saw in saltwater aquariums.

"It's a whole new world under the surface." Joe handed her another photo. "Your grandmother was a natural, took to snorkeling like a duck to water. We should call her the diving duck." He reached over and patted Gran's hand. "When we go again, we'll take Shawna, too. She'd love it." He checked his watch. "We better get going, darlin'. I've got first watch tomorrow."

DJ hugged her stomach with both arms. Anything to keep it in place. *Stay here, Gran. Don't leave me again.* But instead, she smiled and waved goodbye from the lighted doorway.

Then headed for her bedroom at a run.

The next morning, everyone hurried through their chores. DJ spent an hour and a half with Patches, making sure she focused on him entirely. He could get out of control faster than any horse she'd known, but when he decided to cooperate, he learned quickly and never forgot the lesson.

"I think the trick with him is to let him work off all his steam on the hot walker. Either that or just take him around the ring until he settles down." Bridget had been watching the last few minutes of the session. "He has too much energy. But you are doing a good job with him."

"I don't want his riders to get frightened at first, especially the child." DJ leaned forward and stroked Patches' mane away from where it had tangled in the headstall.

"The boy is going to ride Bandit at first, like you suggested. Think I will put him in your beginners' class."

"But the others are already riding well."

"He will catch up with some extra coaching. You will have him on Mondays and Wednesdays at first, then right before your girls, then with them. It will work." Bridget turned to leave. "Johnsons aren't interested in showing; they want to trail-ride as a family. Or at least that is what they are saying now."

DJ dismounted and led Patches out of the arena.

"You get an extra treat today. You've been a good boy."
As soon as she stripped the tack off, she fed him a horse
cookie, brushed him down, and led him out to the hot
walker.

James was just saddling up. "You got him looking
good, DJ."

"Thanks. What's happening?"

James finished buckling the girth on his flat saddle.
"This is my last day here."

"What?"

"Gray Bar and I both leave tomorrow for Virginia."
He ducked his head, fiddling with the stirrups.

"Oh, James, no."

"I gotta get her worked." James kept his head turned
toward the horse when he pushed by DJ.

"We'll still be here when you come home for the summer." She tried to sound cheerful, as if leaving for a military academy was the most natural thing in the world.

"You may be, but my house won't. Mom and Dad are
selling it. I don't even know who I'm going to live with—
or where."

Was that the sheen of a tear on his cheek? She turned
away so he wouldn't be more embarrassed. What could
she say? "Bridget asked me to tell you to come up to the
office as soon as you're finished." DJ crammed her hands
into her pockets. Here she'd been feeling sorry for herself because Gran now lived with Joe, and James didn't
even know who he was going to live with. Bummer. Double bummer.

"I'll see."

"You better—she sounded determined."

"What did I do now?"

"Got me." DJ turned away again, this time to hide a

smile. She knew what Bridget wanted. All the student workers did except for James.

"Surprise! Surprise!" everyone hollered when James walked through the door.

He stopped as though he'd walked into a glass wall. His face turned as red as the helium balloons bobbing on strings tied to the chairs and table legs. He half turned as if to run back out the door he had just come in.

"Come on, James." DJ stepped in his way. She kept her voice low for his ears only. "You can do this."

He turned back. "Th-thanks. How come no one told me?"

Giggles broke out. "It's a surprise party, that's why!"

"Okay, everyone, line up over here for hot dogs, then get the rest of your food." One of the mothers working behind the food table called out, "James, you get to be first since you're the guest of honor."

Hilary nudged James forward. "Come on, we're starved. I didn't have lunch yet because of you, so get with it." The grin she wore lit up her dark eyes. "We really surprised you, didn't we?"

James nodded. He picked up a paper plate and asked for two hot dogs.

Before long everyone had a plateful and had found a place to sit. In between bites, talk of the Labor Day horse show took over. DJ, Amy, James, and a couple of others sat cross-legged on the floor in a circle.

"So you'll be involved in the horse program at your new school?" one of them asked.

James nodded, his mouth full of food. "I want to get on the novice jumping team. And I can ride on fox hunts in the fall."

"Cool." One of the other boys leaned back and thumped James on the arm. "Then you could compete hunter/jumper. Just think, riding behind hounds. I watched 'em do it in a movie once. Incredible."

"Yeah, I guess."

DJ studied James from under her eyelashes. Just a few weeks ago he was the biggest pain in her life, and now they were friends. Incredible was the word all right. And she knew who to thank. Only God worked miracles.

After the cake was served, Bridget clapped for order. She brought a wrapped package out from under her desk and handed it to James. "So you do not forget us. You will be a success at that Academy. You are really just exchanging one academy for another. And they will not be any tougher than I am, you can count on it."

"Th-thanks." He tore into the paper and held up a black T-shirt. Inside a circle of white letters that read *Briones Academy*, a white horse and rider cleared a triple.

"You now have the first shirt produced for our school here. The rest of my students will have to buy theirs." Bridget handed him another box. "This one is from everybody."

James lifted a shiny new headstall out of the box. "Thank you." His voice cracked on the words.

DJ leaped to her feet and started picking up dirty plates and plastic cups. "Come on, you guys, put away your mess." She knew how James felt, hating to cry and so afraid he might. And one look at his face told her how close he was.

Saying goodbye when you didn't know if you'd ever see that person again was the pits. "I'll write if you will." She helped James find all his gear in the tack room.

"You got a modem?" James dug a brush with his name on it out of the tack box.

"No, I don't even have a computer. Why?"

"I could send you messages that way." James found an old jacket in the closet. "Faster and easier than the post office."

"Sorry, you'll have to use the mail. Or the phone." She picked up a loaded bucket and lugged it over to Gray Bar's stall. "You learn to jump, old girl, and I'll see you in the ring next year." She stroked the filly's nose and rubbed her ears. "See ya." She turned, gave James a hug, and hustled out the door. What she wouldn't give to tell his parents what a mess they were making of their kid's life. Military school! It was all so stupid.

Tuesday morning her eyes flew open and she leaped out of bed. No more restrictions. She was free! She could use the phone, watch TV, visit Amy. . . . Today she would ride Megs again—and this evening, Joe was taking her to meet Major, her soon-to-be own horse.

"I'm free!" she sang to Amy when she came out the door of her house.

"Do you have to be free so early in the morning?" Amy tried to grumble, but ended up grinning instead. "You get to jump again."

"And tonight I get to see Major. What a day! What a super fantastical, awesome day." DJ raised her face to the sun peeping over the tops of the buckeye and euca-lyptus trees. "Nothing can stop me now—I'm on my way. Olympics, here I come!"

"You might want to win a couple local shows and

qualify for the Grand National first." The two pedaled side by side up the street.

"Gran always says you need the dream first. Can't you just imagine?" DJ flung her arms straight out, causing her bike to waver from side to side.

"I can imagine you splattered all over the street if you don't watch out."

"Amy Marie Yamamoto, you are the most—"

"Most perfect friend you've ever had."

"Right." DJ's thoughts flitted to James. Wouldn't it be awful to have to move away and leave your friends behind? Especially a friend like Amy. They'd been best friends since preschool. Poor James, his flight left at 7:00 A.M. She glanced at her watch—right about now.

They parked their bikes beside the barn and checked the duty board. Who would take over James' chores? Two new names appeared on the roster. Tony Andrada and Rachel Jones.

DJ and Amy swapped raised-eyebrow looks. "Sure hope they know how to work. We just got James whipped into shape before he left. Is Tony a girl or guy?"

"Got me. I've never met either of them." DJ's gaze scanned the board. "But Hilary is training them, so I don't have to. And look, they're taking some of my stalls. Good deal!"

"So what'll you do?"

DJ shrugged. "Who knows—besides Bridget, that is. But I'm sure she has something planned. Today I have stalls, Patches, my lesson—my lesson!" She threw her hands in the air and jigged around in a circle. "I finally get to jump again!"

"It hasn't been forever, you know."

"Just seems like it." She did another jig step.

"You know, DJ, one thing I like about you is your low-key personality." Bridget stopped just inside the door. The smile on her face made DJ feel as though the sun shone inside the building. "You get Megs saddled, and I will meet you in the arena in ten minutes?"

"I'm outta here." DJ dashed across to the barn and saddled Megs in record time. Once in the ring and mounted up, she wanted to whoop and shout. Even staid Megs caught the excitement and pranced to the side. "Thank you, thank you, thank you, God!" Her words kept time with the slow trot, one hoofbeat per word.

She felt as if she were flying. When Megs left the ground to clear each jump, DJ was sure they were going to take off and circle like Pegasus. They could have easily cleared a brush and pole or a square oxer if they'd been in the arena.

"DJ, that was an excellent performance. I could tell Megs was having as much fun as you were. When the rider is confident, the horse will do far beyond its best. Remember what this felt like and how you feel right now. Dream about it and know you can recapture this feeling. The best riding is as much mental as physical."

"I think this was the most fun I've had in my entire life." DJ leaned forward and hugged Megs with both arms. "You old sweetie. Thank you, Megs."

Her class went the same way.

"That was fun, DJ." Sam stopped her horse by the open gate. "I wish school wouldn't start for months or ever. I love it here." She leaned forward and rubbed her horse's neck. "When are we going back up in Briones?"

"After what we went through, you want to go back?"

"Sure." Angie stopped beside her. "A stupid ol' bee can't keep us away."

"Well, we'll see."

"Now you sound just like a grown-up." Krissie shook her head. "And we thought you were different."

DJ took hold of the girl's bridle. "Get back to the barn before your mother scolds me for taking too long. You want to get me in trouble?"

They shook their heads and headed for the barn, giggles floating back over their shoulders.

After the girls finished grooming their horses and cleaning their stalls, Mrs. Lincoln returned to pick up Angie. She handed a wrapped package to Angie, who brought it to DJ with a smile big enough to crack her face.

"Here, we want you to have this—kind of a thank-you."

"For what?" DJ looked from Angie to her mother.

"For saving my daughter's life."

"Yeah, but . . ." DJ sputtered the words. "You . . . you can't—"

"Yes, we can. Just open it." Mrs. Lincoln clasped her hands on her mountain of a stomach.

DJ tore the paper and let it drop to her feet. Inside the box lay a headstall and reins, along with an envelope. "Wow, what a beauty."

"For your new horse." Angie crowded close. "Open the envelope."

Inside was a gift certificate for a local tack shop.

"We thought you could use that for a bit. We didn't know what kind to buy." Angie looked up at DJ. "Do you like it?"

"Like it. I don't know what to say. Thank you."

"Thank *you*, DJ. Your quick thinking made me feel so much braver about letting Angie out of my sight. The first time she got stung by a bee, we found out she had asthma. Until then, we thought her breathing problems were only allergies." Mrs. Lincoln tried to straighten and twisted her shoulders from side to side. "I have an ache in my lower back that tells me we better get home. We might have a baby tonight."

"Are you sure you can drive?" DJ asked. "I mean— should you? I can call someone."

"No, no. It'll be hours yet, and maybe not till tomorrow. But I probably won't make the show this weekend." She patted DJ on the shoulder. "See you."

DJ watched them get in their car and leave. *What an incredible thing for them to do.* She held the headstall in her hand, running her fingers over the smooth leather. It looked large enough for a big horse, all right. And Joe had said Major was more than sixteen hands tall.

When she took Patches out in the arena, even *he* behaved—for him anyway. He tried to run away with her only once.

She didn't even mind the empty house when she got home. Joe would be coming soon!

8

"MAJOR, I'D LIKE YOU to meet my new grand-daughter, Darla Jean Randall. She prefers to be called DJ."

"Oh, wow." DJ stretched out her hand so the big horse could sniff her. "Major, am I ever glad to meet you." She smiled at the tickle of his whiskers on the back of her hand and up her arm. He continued his sniffing exploration, up her shoulder, her hair. When he gently blew horsy breath in her face, she knew she was accepted.

DJ dug in her pocket for the bit of carrot and the horse cookie she'd brought along. She held them out, one on each palm. "Which do you like best?"

Major looked at her, intelligence beaming from his large, dark eyes. He nosed each treat, then lipped the carrot first.

"Ah, so you're a vegetable man." He quickly ate the other before she changed her mind and put it away.

"He likes sugar the best, but I keep telling him cubes aren't good for his teeth." Joe rubbed up behind the black ears and down the horse's neck and shoulder. "But you don't agree, do you, old man?" Major leaned into the rubbing, almost purring in pleasure.

"What else does he like?"

"Popcorn, peanuts, candy. When we're out on patrol, he's not supposed to have snacks, but sometimes kids sneak him things. He likes kids, hates guns, and has a heart as big as the Golden Gate Bridge."

DJ rubbed the horse's cheek and stroked the white blaze down his face. When she stopped, Major ducked his head lower so she could reach him more easily.

"He loves parades, especially when the mounted police march as a unit. Crowd control is what he excels at. Not too many people argue when he swings his rump around and moves to the side. See his feet? While he's careful where he puts them, even the roughest, drunkest agitators don't want to get their feet stepped on."

"But he doesn't have big feet for his size."

"No, but he looks as though he could mash your foot, wouldn't you say?"

DJ nodded. "Even a pony stepping right on your toes can hurt."

"Right. And you should see Major when he pins his ears to his head and starts to glare. Could melt ice, he could." Joe stepped back. "He and I, we've been through many a scrape, we have." He retrieved a lead rope off the nail by the horse's stall and snapped it to the blue nylon halter. "Here, I'll take him out so you can see how he moves. Sorry, I can't let you ride him tonight, department regulations, you know."

"That's okay. What breed did you say he was?"

"Morgan-Thoroughbred. Half and half. Nice easy gaits; you can ride him all day and not get tired. I should know, I have." He led the horse down the dirt aisle.

DJ stood and watched the horse's action from the

rear. Strong in the haunches, straight in the leg. She tried to remember all the points Bridget had been teaching her. He was a good mover; it showed in knees, hocks, and ankles. Bridget said that was important for a jumper. That and strength in the hindquarters.

"You say he likes to jump?"

"When he's had a chance. We set up some low jumps over a downed tree in Golden Gate Park a couple times for fun. He learns quickly and remembers better'n an elephant. If he gets a treat at a certain place one time, he'll expect it every time."

Joe stopped Major right in front of DJ. He held the gelding at attention, head up, ears forward, feet squared. The white blaze down the horse's face gleamed in the light from the overhead bar.

DJ smoothed her hand down the horse's shoulder and down his leg. When her hand ran over his fetlock, Major lifted his foot without any hesitation. DJ moved to the rear and checked each of his legs. The horse obeyed the slightest command. "He's had to learn to be handled by more than one person; police horses can't be picky about their riders. It's just he and I've been on the force together for so long, he became mine."

She let Major sniff her shoulder again before working down the last leg. Halfway down his shoulder lay a patch of black skin with no hair. "What happened here?"

"That was a bullet meant for me. He deflected the shot by running into the guy. Not much of a scar left now, but that was too close a call for either of us." Joe smoothed the sleek hair down over the spot. "His badge of honor."

"Wow. When you said he was all heart, you weren't kiddin'." DJ stood back to look at the horse face on.

Deep, wide chest and balanced on all fours. "He sure looks good to me. How do you get your horses here?"

"We purchase some, but many are donated. A calm temperament is most important. We also like it when we can form a drill with matching horses—bays like Major here are popular. I was fortunate that when I needed a horse, a family was moving to the East Coast and needed a home for their horse." He stroked the arched neck with obvious love. "Major and I've been buddies ever since."

This is going to be my horse as soon as Joe retires. DJ felt like dancing again. Like running up and throwing her arms around the bay's neck, then hugging Joe. Or maybe the other way around.

"Do you like him?" The question caught her short.

"*Like* him? How could I not like him? I just can't understand why you want to sell him."

Joe put the horse back into his stall and unsnapped the lead. "Well, it's like this. I decided to buy him and keep him for my grandchildren to ride. I knew Shawna had horses on the brain, and I thought maybe Bobby and Billy might like to ride someday. That way I could keep my best friend here with me. He's too young to be put out to pasture."

DJ stroked the horse one more time, told him good-night, and followed Joe down the aisle. They waved good-night to the officer on duty and the night watchman.

"So why sell him to me?"

"Are you sure you want him?

"Joe, for pete's sake, what do I have to do—get down on my knees and beg?" DJ shot him a questioning look. What was wrong with the man? Couldn't he see she was already nuts about the horse?

"Okay." He opened the car door for her. "I know he'll be good for you."

"So?"

"All my life I've dreamed of having a cutting horse. Goes back to my love of Western movies, I guess. You know, where the cowboy and his horse are cutting cows out of the herd and the horse saves the rider from an irate bull. That kind of thing." Joe ducked his chin, as if embarrassed to admit his dream.

"Hey, that's cool."

"Since you'll be putting Major to work, I'm going to buy a cutting horse and enter the competitions. Think your grandmother will tag along while I compete?"

"Sure." DJ shrugged. "Long as she doesn't have a deadline. Gran will try anything and have a ball doing it."

"Does Bridget know anything about cutting horses?"

"Some. She knows something about all kinds of horses and lots about showing and jumping. She'll put you in touch with the right people."

Joe eased his car into traffic on the Bay Bridge. "Kind of exciting finally realizing a lifelong dream—my cutting horse, I mean."

"Tell me about it. I've wanted a horse of my own since I was little. I started working at the Academy when I was ten so I could have riding lessons. Mom and Gran thought I'd quit in a couple weeks." DJ couldn't believe she was talking like this with the man who had stolen Gran. It wasn't long ago that she'd decided to hate him.

"Melanie says you want to jump in the Olympics someday."

"Yep, that's my dream." It seemed strange to hear Gran referred to as anything but Gran. Melanie was someone else entirely. "I have a long way to go, so much to learn."

"That's what makes life interesting." Joe checked over his shoulder and changed lanes. "You up for an ice cream sundae?"

"Sure. There's a good place in Pleasant Hill. I'll show you where to turn." DJ looked over at the man driving the car. Light from the dashboard showed a strong face with an almost permanent smile. Laugh lines crinkled the edges of his sky blue eyes. His thick hair looked more white than gray in the dimness. It was cut short as though he didn't care to fuss with it.

"You think I could compete with a cutting horse?"

"Why not? There are all kinds of local shows. If the horse is really good and you don't feel confident enough, you can hire someone to train and show him."

Joe nodded. "I mentioned to your grandmother that I might be too old to do something like this, and she nearly bit my head off."

"A lot of retired people compete. They've finally got a chance to buy a horse, and they're loving it." DJ pointed to a huge plastic balloon shaped like an ice cream container. "Over there. Take the next exit."

By the time they finished their ice cream and Joe dropped her off at home, DJ knew she had a friend for life. Of course, their love for horses gave them plenty to talk about. Joe Crowder was an easy man to talk to. No wonder Gran had fallen in love so fast.

DJ fell asleep thanking God for the big horse that had already taken over a large part of her heart. Soon Major would be hers!

She talked nonstop on the way to the Academy in the

morning, telling Amy all about the dark bay horse and her evening with Joe.

"And you didn't want Gran to marry him." Amy set the kickstand on her bike.

"I know. Maybe I could go live with Gran and Joe." She'd thought that before, but never said it out loud.

"DJ, you already have a home."

"Yeah." DJ thought back to the empty house she'd gladly left behind. If she didn't get a bunch of housework done today, she and her mother would be at it again. How come one house could get so messed up with only two people living in it?

Patches pranced around the hot walker, his momentum dragging the other horses clipped to it along at a trot. DJ stopped to watch him for a second. He sure was lively today. She hustled back to the barn to clean his stall. Bridget had increased her time with the gelding to two hours on the days she wasn't teaching.

Once in the arena, she trotted him around the circle three or four times, waiting for the signal that he was ready to settle down to business. When he finally agreed to an easy jog, she knew the time was right.

"Boy, whoever rides you is going to have to spend plenty of time in the warm-up arena." She patted his neck and started him into the routine. Figure eights for reining, first at a walk, then a jog, and finally a lope. He learned to dance with her as they practiced lead changes around the ring. Her body swayed with the rhythm— lean left, left lead; lean right, right lead. The movements gentle, the lope a thing of beauty and grace.

"Good Patches. That was the best ever." She reined him to a halt and patted his neck. There was no better feeling in the world than when a horse did what he was asked. She took in a breath scented with dust and the horse beneath her. "Okay, next step. Time to learn to back up."

She dismounted and, with the reins in one hand, tapped his shoulder with the other and pulled back with the reins. "Back, Patches, back," she instructed. Patches shifted from side to side and snorted. DJ repeated the command, voice firm, "Back, Patches, back."

This time he backed away from the pull on his bit. "Good job, Patches." She patted him and rubbed his nose. When she repeated the command, he planted his feet and didn't budge.

"Fiddle. And here I thought you were going to get this right away." She settled him down and tried again. Patches laid his ears back.

DJ took a deep breath, calming herself as much as the horse. The next time, he swished his tail, but he backed up a couple of steps. "Good, fella." This time he got loves and pats. He rubbed his nose against her shoulder.

When he obeyed the command four times in a row, DJ decided it was time to try the same command from his back. She mounted and settled into the saddle. "Back, Patches, back." She gently but firmly pulled back on the reins and leaned forward slightly, leaving the back door open for him to follow the command. "Back, Patches, back." He flattened his ears back and shifted from one foot to the other before he twitched his tail and backed up. DJ thumped on his neck and down his shoulder. "Good fella, Patches. Good." She petted him for a few moments, then gave the command again.

When he had obeyed three times in a row without arguing, she nudged him forward and let him jog around the arena. He let out a relieved-sounding snort.

"I'm with you, fella. But you did good." Just as she leaned forward to stroke his neck, a little kid ran up to the fence and leaped on the rails, his shoes clanging on the aluminum bars.

Patches exploded. Head down, rear feet in the air. Stiff-legged hop and another buck.

DJ grabbed for the saddle horn. Too late. She was off and flying through the air.

She hit the dirt with a *thwump* that vibrated throughout her body.

9

AIR. I CAN'T GET AIR.

"DJ, are you okay?"

If I could breathe, I might be. DJ fought the clenching pain in her chest. She wiggled her fingers and toes. Yep, all there and working. It was just her breath. She tried to take little shallow huffs. Getting the wind knocked out of you took some getting used to.

She looked up to find Amy peering down into her face.

"Blink if you can hear me." Amy spoke slowly, as if DJ were hard of hearing.

DJ blinked.

"Hey, you know what? You're supposed to tuck and roll on a fall like that, not land flat out."

DJ's furious gaze made Amy grin.

"Are you really all right?" Amy let her concern show.

"I . . . am . . . fine." The whisper broke through the lock on DJ's chest. "Wh-where . . . is . . . P. . . ?"

"Running around like a wild mustang. Hilary and John are trying to catch him."

"I . . . could . . . k . . ." DJ finally was able to get enough air past her tongue to talk. She pushed herself

85

till she was sitting on one hip, her straight arms propping her up. Her head refused to remain upright without a steel brace, but other than that, she thought she might live. At least live long enough to kill that . . . She halted the thought. Calling him names wouldn't do anyone any good. And at the moment it was a waste of good air.

"You're really all right?"

"I will be." DJ sucked in a deep breath and spit out the grains of dirt that coated her lips. She rubbed them together, then backhanded her mouth. "That good-for-nothing horse, I . . ." She looked around the arena to spot him playing dodge 'em with the two workers.

"I think he's laughing." Amy fought now to keep a straight face.

"Well, don't *you* laugh. I'll find my sense of humor again, after I beat him into the ground." DJ reached out a hand and let Amy pull her up. Standing, her chest still hurt, but she no longer sounded like a leaky bellows. She dusted off her jeans and T-shirt.

"You look like you've been rolling around in the dirt." Amy ducked a left swing. "How you gonna catch Patches?"

"The only way. Get a grain bucket." DJ strode off across the arena and out the gate, calling Patches all the names she could think of and a few she made up as she went along. She included a few for herself as well.

"That won't help." Bridget met her halfway back across the parking lot.

"The grain won't? Sure it will, he loves treats."

"No, calling yourself names. Getting dumped sometimes just goes with the territory." Bridget kept pace with DJ.

"How'd you know?"

"DJ, anyone can read your face like an open book. Besides, I remember the times it happened to me. You always think you could have done something differently. Maybe you could have. You never know what will happen to spook a horse, so you need to do your best to pay attention, build lightning reflexes, and dust yourself off when you hit the ground. Praying that you do not get hurt is not a bad idea, either."

DJ nodded. "Here I was patting him and telling him what a great job he was doing, and he dumped me. See if he ever gets praise from me again." Her smile said she was teasing.

She let herself into the arena and shook the bucket. "Hey, Patches, how about lunch?"

Hilary and John both gave her a grateful look. The ones they directed at the now-calming horse could have branded him with a big *D* for disgusting. Patches trotted over to DJ and stuck his head out to sniff the bucket. DJ poured grain from her hand back into the pail. Patches stepped closer. DJ reached out and snagged his reins with one hand, letting him grab a bite before handing the pail to Amy. "There now, mister, your running days are done."

"Get back on him now and make him go through his paces so he does not think he can get away with this type of behavior." Bridget crossed her arms on the top rail and rested her chin on a closed fist.

DJ did as ordered, feeling some creaks in her body when she swung her leg over the saddle. It might be a good idea to take a long, hot soak when she got home. Shame they didn't have a hot tub.

She kept a careful eye on her horse and worked him through walk, jog, lope, figure eights, and reverses, working about five feet from the rail. The first time he came to the spot where the child had scared him, he tried to leap clear across the arena—without touching the ground. DJ moved right with him, ready and waiting for his antics.

"Good, that's the way. Do not ever let a horse buffalo you. Show him who is in control."

"He's come a long way, hasn't he?" Mrs. Johnson said when she joined Bridget and DJ at the fence a few minutes later. "But I can certainly see why he isn't a horse for Andrew here. I'm glad I'm not the one training him, even though I've ridden in the past."

"Once DJ is finished with Patches, he'll be a dependable horse for you."

"Maybe we should have you watch for a large pony for us, something more like Bandit." The woman smoothed a strand of long blond hair back into the club at her neck. She dropped her hand to the shoulder of the slender boy standing beside her.

DJ watched the boy's reaction. He didn't look as though learning to ride was the thing he wanted most in the world. In fact, he looked scared to bits. *Uh-oh*, she thought. *This could be a hard one*.

"How would you like to pet Patches?" she asked the silent child. While he looked to be about eight, his face had the pallor of a child who spent most of his time indoors. Had he been sick or something?

Andrew shook his head.

"Come on, dear." Mrs. Johnson took her son's hand and reached toward the horse's muzzle with it.

Patches lowered his head and sniffed, then snorted, not even a big snort.

Andrew jerked back.

Patches jerked up.

DJ knew they were in trouble. His lesson today would not be on a horse's back—not even one as gentle as Bandit.

"Let me put Patches here away, and then we'll start our lesson," she said with a smile meant to reassure the child.

Even she could tell the smile had failed. This kid did *not* want anything to do with horses.

When DJ put the gelding back in his stall, he rubbed his forehead against her chest and blew gently, as if he was worn out. "You silly thing. Yes, I forgive you. Just don't do it again, okay?" Patches snuffled her cheek and nosed her pocket, obviously hoping for a treat.

"Sorry, fella, you don't deserve one. I'm fresh out anyway." She slid the lower half of the door in place and headed for the drink machine. She'd earned a can of root beer, that was for sure. Then it was on to Andrew.

But when the boy absolutely refused to leave his mother's side, Mrs. Johnson smiled apologetically and sent Andrew to the car. He scampered off as if shot from a cannon. "I'm sure he'll come around. We'll be back on Tuesday."

"From now on she will not be allowed in the area while you are giving a lesson." Bridget patted DJ on the shoulder. "I will take care of that, and you can help that scared little rabbit learn horses can be good friends."

DJ nodded, but felt doubtful.

Sipping her drink, she wandered back to the tack room and gathered her grooming supplies. Even though she didn't have many stalls to clean, she still had a couple horses to groom.

When DJ got home, a message on the machine from

Angie said she had a new baby brother. DJ clapped her hands. "All right!" She found the note her mother had left that morning, including a long list of chores to do. Lindy would be late tonight, and she had to leave on an unexpected trip in the morning. DJ felt her chin bounce to the floor and refuse to return to its proper place. So what was *she* supposed to do? Could she stay by herself? Why not? She wandered around the house, touching Gran's easel, her wing chair. DJ picked up Gran's painting smock and raised it to her nose. The bite of turpentine and the smell of paints were mingled with the floral fragrance that was Gran. DJ dropped the garment back on its hook on the edge of the easel.

She'd better get to vacuuming. The cord was tangled around the broom in the closet, and when she jerked on the handle, a bundle of cleaning rags scattered at her feet. Putting them back caused the mop to fall over.

"This kind of thing only happens in cartoons." DJ slammed the door on the mess and headed for the kitchen. Fixing a snack sounded like a better idea. But her breakfast stuff, along with her mother's, still cluttered the counter.

"How come I have to pick up after her, too?" DJ grumbled at the food containers in the open fridge. She pushed things around until she found the pickle slices, took them out along with the mayo and lettuce, and set them on the counter. After making a ham and cheese sandwich, she added chips to her plate and took it into the family room. She could watch television now that she was off restrictions, so she plunked down in a corner of the sofa, raised the remote, and started flipping channels.

Channel surfing drove her mother nuts. DJ kept

pressing the button just for the pure fun of it, even though she didn't really like it either—at least not when someone else was doing it. Nothing worth watching unless it was Oprah. She tuned it in for a moment, then flicked the off button. She was done with lunch anyway.

By the time she'd finished the chores her mother had assigned her, the sun had sunk behind the trees. DJ settled into the lounge on the deck with a root beer and her sketch pad, but she couldn't keep her mind on drawing.

Could she stay alone while her mother traveled? Of course. Did she want to? The house seemed so empty in the daylight, what would it be like at midnight? *It doesn't make any difference—I'd be asleep by then.*

Mom would never let her stay alone. She could go to Amy's. If only Gran was living here where she belonged rather than in San Francisco. Here DJ was fourteen years old, and she'd never stayed alone all night.

"Grow up, you can't be a baby all your life." House finches chirped and tweeted in the buckeye tree by the side fence. Mourning doves dug in the seeds at the bottom of the feeder, their wings whistling when they flew. The backyard peace settled around her. A couple of blocks over, the Rottweiler barked, his deep voice announcing his family's homecoming.

"Gran, you need to be here. You're the one who made our backyard so perfect. What will happen to it without you?" DJ knew she should turn on the sprinklers. The lawn needed mowing. How was she supposed to take care of the house, the yard, work at the Academy, and return to school next week? How was she going to make it?

The questions stole the gentle peace and sent her mind into overdrive. She glared at her sketch pad. The horse she'd been drawing while she'd been thinking was off kilter; something was wrong with his shoulders and the way he carried his head. She crisscrossed angry lines right through him.

She looked up to see Lindy standing on the deck. "Did you call Gran and ask if she could come stay with you?" her mother asked as she sorted the mail. Obviously the stack of bills hadn't helped her mood any.

"No."

"Did you ask Amy if you could stay there?"

"No." DJ softened her tone. "I've been thinking, it's only one night, and since I'm fourteen now, I should be able to stay alone."

"Over my dead body."

"M-o-ther. Other people my age stay alone."

"Not my kid." Lindy headed for the phone. "I'll call Gran. I have to be gone two days next week, too. Have to fly down to Los Angeles on Monday night for a meeting at eight Tuesday morning."

DJ may have looked as if she were listening to her mother, but the voices inside her head were arguing so loudly, she couldn't hear anything else. She clamped her teeth together to keep them from coming out.

This was so unfair.

"Gran said she'll come." Lindy returned to the family room where DJ sat crossways in a chair, her legs dangling over the side. She'd chewed two nails down to the quick.

"Great, treat me like a baby. See if I care."

"Darla Jean, what has gotten into you?" Her mother planted her feet in the carpet and her hands on her hips—right smack in front of DJ. "I know you hate being here alone in the afternoon and evening, so why the big push for all night?"

"I have to grow up sometime. You keep telling me to grow up, and then when I try, you call Gran. 'Please, Mom, come take care of our little darling.' " DJ imitated her mother's voice to perfection. The sneer on her face was her own.

"If you can't talk any more politely than that, you may go to your room."

"Gladly." DJ shoved herself out of the chair and stormed past her mother, thudding her fury out on each stairstep. Just in time, she thought the better of slamming her door. She could barely hear the click of the lock over the pounding of the blood in her head.

She locked her arms across her chest and stared out the window, angry with herself for losing her temper again.

This was all so stupid. She really hadn't wanted to stay alone, and now she had made a big issue out of it. Maybe the fall from Patches had rattled her brains, too.

Gran was in the kitchen the next afternoon when DJ returned from her day at the Academy. DJ crossed the tile floor and wrapped both arms around her grandmother, inhaling the wonderful floral fragrance that Gran had worn so long it seemed steeped in her pores.

"I've missed you so, darlin', you just can't imagine." Gran hugged both arms around DJ's waist.

"Try me. Nothing's the same without you here." DJ stepped back and looked her grandmother in the face. "You don't have to do this, you know. I could stay by myself."

"Oh, I think Joe can live one night without me. He has two days off next week, so we'll both stay here then."

"You'll be here when school starts." Joy welled up and splashed across DJ's face.

The two of them spent the evening out in the backyard, pruning the roses, staking the chrysanthemums, and digging out the bent grass that tried to take over everything.

DJ pointed up at two hummingbirds playing buzz tag, each trying to chase the other out of the yard. One perched on a branch of the pink oleander, then rose up clicking his warning when the other returned.

DJ sat on the grass, her arms crossed over her raised knees. This was the way it was supposed to be. Her and Gran.

"Gran?"

"Yes, dear?" Gran looked up from where she was plucking dead flower heads off the red geranium.

"Can I come and live with you and Joe? When you move into your house out here, I mean."

10

"OH, MY DEAR, IS IT THAT BAD?"

DJ studied her chewed-off fingernails. "Mom and I just don't get along too well—you know that." She raised her gaze to see her grandmother shaking her head.

"I know. Maybe it's all my fault." Gran sank down on the grass beside DJ.

"How could it be your fault? You're the one who took care of me." DJ crossed her legs and propped her elbows on her knees.

"Yes, and I took over your mother's job. It seemed best at the time, but now I'm not so sure."

"Gran, that's not what I meant." DJ wished she could bite off her tongue. Why'd she ever bring this up? "Don't feel bad, please. I wouldn't hurt you for the world."

"I know, darlin'. I know." Gran reached over and laid a hand on DJ's upper arm. "We'll all just have to pray about this, let God make it better. He will, you know, if you ask."

"I asked. Mom and I really had a big fight then." DJ eyed a hanging cuticle. Her hand automatically rose to her mouth so she could chew it off. A bit of garden dirt came with it. She spit that out.

Gran took DJ's hand in hers and clucked over the mangled fingernails. "Oh, darlin'." Her voice felt as soft as the falling twilight.

DJ pulled her hand back. "I've been praying about my fingernails, too, and look where it's got me."

"I know. Satan seems to jump right in and let us have it with both barrels as soon as we pray for help changing something. But God's Word is stronger, mightier than a sword." Gran rose to her feet. "Come on, we have to find just the right verse for you. Then when you start to chew your nails, you repeat the Bible verse until the need to chew is gone."

"Oh, right, Gran. You won't find a verse about fingernails." DJ got up and, after picking up their gardening tools and dumping the weeds and trimmings in the compost bin, followed Gran into the house.

Gran had settled into her wing chair, Bible on her lap. A pad of paper and pencil lay beside her on the lamp table.

DJ leaned closer to read the writing on the tablet. Psalm 139 stood out at the top of the list. She looked up into Gran's face. The light from the lamp created a halo in the gold-shot fluffy hair. A halo sure did fit Gran. If anyone was an angel, it was her.

DJ took her usual position at Gran's feet, her cheek resting against Gran's knee. Immediately Gran laid a hand on DJ's head and stroked, much like DJ did with her horses. Calming, comforting, and full of love.

DJ's sigh started at her toes and slithered its way to her head. If only they could go back to the way things used to be. She blinked. Did she want to go back? Back before Joe? Before Major? She scrunched her eyes shut.

"Why don't you and Joe live here? Then everything would be just fine."

"I'm glad you want to keep him in the family. He thinks you're pretty special, too, you know." Gran kept up the stroking.

"I had a great time with him on Tuesday. He's real easy to talk to." DJ tilted her head so the stroking hand could soothe a new place.

"I know. He laughs easily, knows how to have a good time, and gives God the glory for everything—including meeting me and my family."

DJ flinched. Thinking back to the way she'd behaved before the wedding made her want to crawl under the rug. Gran stopped stroking to write down another reference.

"I'll give you this list in the morning. How about scrambled eggs for breakfast?"

"Okay." DJ stood up, her yawn nearly cracking her jaw. "Good-night." She bent down to give Gran a hug and a kiss. "Think you can get through the night without seeing Joe?" She dropped another kiss in the middle of Gran's halo.

"Oh, you!" Gran gave her a playful swat. "For your information, I was just about to call him."

"Tell him hi for me." Another yawn, this one longer than the first. She headed for the stairs. How come Gran could make such a difference in the atmosphere of the house?

Two days later, Saturday morning dawned. The birds were barely chirping before DJ was out of bed and scrambling for her clothes. Mr. Yamamoto would be driving her and Amy and all their gear to the Academy. He helped to load horses for all the shows.

A car horn honked. DJ finished gathering her things and flew down the stairs. Maybe by the next show, she'd be able to compete again.

"Morning, DJ. You're looking mighty alert for this time of day," Mr. Yamamoto said out the rolled-down driver's side window. He'd pulled the car into the driveway to turn around.

"Thanks. I love early mornings, unlike someone else we know." DJ opened the rear door and tossed her duffel bag across the seat.

Amy mumbled something from her nest in the front.

"Come on, Ames." DJ settled herself in back. "You can sleep tonight." She thumped her friend on the head.

"Wish there were barns on the showgrounds so we didn't have to trailer the horses every day." DJ pulled a food bar out of her pocket and unwrapped it.

"This is difficult all right." Mr. Yamamoto took a sip from the coffee mug on the dashboard. "I hear you're getting a horse pretty soon."

"Yeah, his name's Major. Wait 'til you see him. He's huge." She took a bite out of her bar. Three-day horse shows took a toll on everyone, both people and horses.

Loading went without a hitch, unlike the time before when Gray Bar caused a ruckus. The thought of Gray Bar made DJ wonder how James was doing. Would he really write?

Once at the Saddle Club grounds, DJ helped the younger riders tie their horses side by side on the long rope stretched from tree to tree. Together, they organized their gear. Parents who hadn't done this before needed as much instruction as their children. They set out grain, then wedges of hay, and DJ showed the kids where to fill the water buckets. She took care of Angie's horse since the girl hadn't shown up yet.

Bridget came by, clipboard in hand. The board held a list of all the academy pupils and the classes they'd entered. She handed DJ a matching board. "Just so we can make changes if needed. And so you can look ahead to see who might need assistance."

"Angie's not here yet."

"They did not ring to say not to bring the horse, so they will be here." Bridget answered a shout from across the long string of horses. "Talk to you later. Any questions, you know how to find me."

"Who does all this stuff when I'm showing?" DJ muttered an hour later.

"We take turns." Hilary stopped brushing her horse long enough to answer. "You've just made my life easier. How about not showing ever again?" Her teeth gleamed white against her dark skin.

"Oh, yeah, I'll just go along to make sure none of you prima donnas have to scoop poop." DJ fetched the shovel from behind Hilary's horse.

"Thank you. I am glad you're getting Major soon. I can't wait 'til we're competing in the same classes. That'll be fun."

"That won't be for a while." DJ waved at one of the fathers who called her name. It was Angie's dad, apologizing for their being late.

Angie was grooming her horse as though she were in a speed competition.

"We had a sick baby last night, and none of us got much sleep." Mr. Lincoln apologized again. "When he finally dropped off, we all did."

"No harm done. Angie, you have plenty of time. Since you're riding Western, you'll be on after noon."

Angie let out a sigh that could be heard clear across the bay to San Francisco. "I want to do good out there, and I can't swallow past my butterflies. Mom was scared I was going to have an asthma attack."

"Oh no. No asthma allowed here. But watch out for the yellow jackets. They come to feast on all the picnic stuff." DJ turned to answer another question. "See ya, Angie. Take it easy."

Angie took third place in her class that afternoon and received a white ribbon to cheering applause from the academy rooting section. Sam got a fourth, and Krissie a sixth.

"Your girls did well. It shows what a good teacher you are." Bridget stopped DJ long enough to give the compliment.

DJ met her girls back at the tie line. "I can't believe it. You guys did super. Wow!"

Their thank-you's and sighs of relief tumbled over each other. The three dismounted and formed a ring with DJ, dancing and hugging.

"You don't get excited or anything, do you?" Amy led her horse past them on her way to the warm-up ring.

"Not a bit." DJ thumped her friend on the arm. "Go get 'em. You have the Academy's honor to uphold."

"Oh, yuk. Thanks a big fat bunch. Now you're making my insides flop around rather than fly in formation."

"Do *you* still get scared?" Angie asked.

"Of course. Everyone gets scared. That's part of showing." Amy led Josh around the arena where the novice Western class was now showing.

By Monday evening when they returned the final trailer load to the Academy, DJ felt as if she'd been dragged under the wheels of the trailers. The academy students, both youth and adult, had done very well. Hilary won hunter/seat equitation again and took a second in hunter/jumper. Amy took the trail-riding class and won two reds and a white in her other events.

"You get on home now; you have done enough," Bridget said when she found DJ putting tack away. "Thank you so much for all your help. You can be proud of yourself. I certainly am."

"Thank you. We did good, didn't we?"

"About the best ever. Our reputation is really growing, thanks to all of you." Bridget turned to leave. "See you tomorrow after school."

DJ groaned. "Thanks for reminding me."

"Hey, you comin'?" Amy trotted up to the tack room. "Dad's ready to go."

As soon as they got into the car, the girls slumped against the doors. Mr. Yamamoto wore a weary look himself.

"Anybody for a pony party?"

Groans drowned out his chuckle.

"Your dad has a sick sense of humor."

"I heard that." Their groans turned to halfhearted giggles. More like wimpy chuckles, really.

"See you at 7:30, right?" he asked after stopping the car at DJ's house. "I see your grandparents are here."

"See ya." Grandparents—as in two. What a nice thought. DJ slung her duffel over her shoulder and dragged herself into the house.

She almost fell asleep trying to tell Joe and Gran about the show.

"Well, I tell you, if you don't have another one before the first of October, this is the last show of yours I miss." Joe crossed one leg over his opposite knee. "I could hardly keep my mind on patrol, I kept thinking of you academy kids competing. Major's going to love it. Today some little kid stuck cotton candy up for him to taste. He tasted it all right. Ate every bit in two bites. The poor kid started screaming. After I gave him money for another cotton candy, I had to take Major to a hose and wash off his face."

DJ giggled at the thought of Major with a pink nose. Her giggle turned into a jaw-cracking yawn. "Mom get off okay?" Gran nodded. DJ yawned again. "I'm so tired I don't think I can climb the stairs."

"Do you have your things ready for the morning?"

"You kidding? This is DJ you're talkin' to, remember? I'll get up early; it's easier than working now." She hugged and kissed Gran, then paused for a second. Crossing to the sofa, she gave Joe a hug, too.

"Night, DJ." Joe sounded gruff, as though maybe he had a frog in his throat. "I'll be at school to pick you up, okay?"

"Great."

"There's something for you up on your desk," Gran said.

DJ gave her a questioning look, but Gran only smiled. The stairs could have been Mt. Everest. DJ groaned when she made it to the top. When she finally dragged her feet down the long hall and into her room, she dumped her bag by the bed and collapsed across it. If only she didn't have to move for ten years.

When she roused herself enough to sit up, her gaze fell on the paper on her desk. In Gran's most beautiful calligraphy, the words leaped off the parchment paper. "I can do all things through Christ who strengthens me."

DJ read the verse through a second time, then a third. So this was her verse to overcome nail-biting, smart-mouthing, and everything else that bugged her. She let the paper float back to the desk. This couldn't really work—could it? Would Gran make up something like this?

Sure, their pastor talked about the power of God's Word, but did God *really* care about Darla Jean Randall chewing her nails? As DJ undressed, she thought about it. If Jesus was really in her heart, and she knew He was, then He cared about every little bit of her. So much He even knew how many hairs were left on her head. Even after she'd left some in the hairbrush that morning.

"You must be awfully smart, God," she muttered as she drew back the covers. "But if you care so much, I'll give it a try. By the way, thanks for taking care of us today. I forget to tell you thank you a lot. Thanks for Joe— he makes Gran so happy. And please help me in school tomorrow. I haven't told anyone else, but I am kind of scared. First day with new teachers and all that stuff is scary." She flipped over on her side and reread the paper. "So that's my verse, huh? Did you put Gran up to this?"

When Mr. Yamamoto let Amy and DJ off in front of the school in the morning, they looked at each other as if they'd rather climb back into the car and head for home. Each girl shrugged her backpack over one shoulder, squared both shoulders, and started out across the parking lot.

"Bye, Dad." Amy turned to wave.

DJ did the same. "Well, let's get to our locker and pick up our class list."

By the end of the day, DJ knew several new things. She and Amy had only one class together. Art would be DJ's favorite, algebra her least. Literature would be fun because she loved to read, and PE would be an easy A. The rest she wasn't sure about. One thing was sure, how was she going to keep up with everything? There was so much she had to do at home and with Major before she'd be ready for the Olympics. How would she ever do it all?

11

"WHO INVENTED SCHOOL ANYWAY?" Amy muttered.

"I don't know, but yell at them for me." DJ slumped against the wall by their shared locker. "And if I don't keep my grades up, you know what will be the first to go."

"You always get straight A's."

"I've never had algebra and Latin before." DJ hoisted her backpack. "Let's see if Joe is waiting for us out there. Mucking fifty stalls would be better than this."

At the Academy she could tell instantly that Bridget and Joe approved of each other. They sized each other up and both turned to smile at DJ. She left the two of them talking about cutting horses and went to saddle Patches.

By the time she'd worked the gelding through his paces and had him backing up smoothly, she could easily forget school ever existed. And once she flew over the jumps with Megs, she felt alive again. This was where she belonged, on a horse, on target for her dream. After she'd groomed Megs, she noticed Hilary frowning at one of the new workers. She had to think a minute before she remembered his name: Tony. He sure didn't look like a happy camper.

"You know these stalls are your responsibility." DJ could tell Hilary was using every ounce of her tact and patience.

What had he done—or not done?

"I cleaned 'em." His lip stuck out far enough to hang a bridle on.

"Then you'll have to clean them again, and do it right this time."

Oh no, not another James. We need a troublemaker like we need manure. DJ felt like calling for Bridget, but they had their code: Handle everything you can yourself. It made you stronger and promoted better feelings between all the student workers.

She turned in time to see Bridget and Joe pause just inside the door.

"You can't make me!" Tony gripped the handle of his shovel.

"No, I can't make you, but I can report you, and then you won't be able to ride or take lessons until Bridget says you can." Hilary leaned against the stall wall as if she didn't have a care in the world. "It's up to you."

Tony glared. He grumbled. He swore. But he went back into the stall and started tossing out dirty shavings.

"Oh, and that kind of language isn't tolerated around here, either, so consider this your warning. I'll be back to check on your progress in half an hour."

DJ sneaked a look at Bridget. The smile of approval she saw on the trainer's face made her more proud of Hilary than she already was. If only she could learn to be so cool under pressure.

She hung up her tack and straightened the bridles.

Hilary came in and sank down on the lid of the tack box.

"You were so cool." DJ sat down beside the older girl.

"Thanks, I felt like taking his shovel and rapping him over the head with it." She shook her head, setting her corn-rowed braids to swinging. "Sometimes I wonder where these jerks come from. Why ask to work here if they don't want to clean stalls?"

"They think it's all show time. The movies don't show how much work goes into caring for horses."

"I guess." Hilary got back up. "Hey, how was school?"

"Don't ask." DJ put on a happy face. "I love my art class, though."

"Sure you do. Let you ride, jump, train, and draw pictures of horses, and you'd be in horse heaven."

"How do you know?"

"'Cause you're just like me." Hilary patted DJ on top of her helmet. "And if you think junior high takes time, wait 'til you hit high school."

As usual, Hilary gave her something to think about.

Gran was ready to put dinner on the table when Joe and DJ walked in the door. "Wash your hands, you two. I don't want any horse hair in my salad." She raised her face for Joe to kiss.

DJ felt a blush start about her collarbone.

"We're embarrassing our girl." Gran pushed the big man away with a gentle hand.

The comment turned the heat up. DJ shook her head at them with a grin. "You're as bad as a couple of teenagers."

"How would you know?"

"I got eyes." Her laughter trailed back as she took the stairs two at a time.

Even with Joe there, dinner felt like it was supposed

to. She and Gran had spent many nights together with Lindy away on business trips. By the time they'd listened to Joe rave about Bridget and the Academy, Gran tell about a new contract, and DJ fill them in on day one at school, darkness had wrapped the house in its comforting arms.

When the phone rang, DJ jumped up to get it. "Hi, Mom. How's your trip going?" DJ twirled the phone cord around her finger while she listened. "Amy and I only have one class together. We don't even have the same lunch. I know I'll live with it, but I'd rather be at the Academy." She grimaced at her mother's response. She should know better than to tease her mother over the phone. "Sure, Gran's here, I'll get her." She put her hand over the mouthpiece and called her grandmother. "See you Wednesday." She handed the phone to Gran, then stopped in the doorway to listen.

"Say, if it's all right, I'd like to have Robert and the boys to dinner on Wednesday," Gran was saying. DJ stopped in surprise. *How come Gran hadn't mentioned it to her?* She headed for the dining room.

"How come you didn't tell me about Wednesday?" She slumped in her chair when Gran came back to the dining room.

"I needed to check it out with your mother first. If you wouldn't eavesdrop like that, you wouldn't discover so many surprises."

DJ slumped lower. She memorized the pattern on her placemat.

"What difference does it make? I just thought this family needed to get to know one another better, and the boys have been begging to come see their cousin." Gran motioned toward the coffeepot, asking Joe if he wanted more.

He shook his head. "I think we're going to have to buy a pony for the grandkids as soon as we move into our house. One like Bandit would be just right."

"Wish we *did* have a pony, we don't have any stuff here to entertain little kids."

"Oh, Robert will bring something. Anyway, the boys love being read to."

"They can sit still long enough for a story?"

Both Gran and Joe laughed at the skeptical look on DJ's face.

"Well, I better hit my books." DJ started stacking dishes to carry to the kitchen.

"You go ahead, I'll get those." Joe stopped her when she reached for his plate.

"Thanks." She dropped a kiss on Gran's head and whispered in her ear. "You better keep him if he does dishes."

"I heard that."

DJ chuckled her way upstairs. "You two just want to smooch without me watching," she yelled down from the top landing.

"Darla Jean, whatever—" Her grandmother's words were cut off.

The more DJ hurried the next afternoon, the more behind she got. Patches was never one to be hurried. His crow-hopping on the backing drill reminded her of that.

By the time she'd taken Megs over the course twice, the mare had refused two jumps.

"All right, DJ, what is bothering you?" Bridget called

from the center of the arena.

"We have company coming for dinner."

"So."

"So I was hurrying."

"And?"

"And hurrying doesn't work. So now I take a deep breath, relax, and take Megs over the course again, concentrating on what I'm doing."

"Good. I can see that you listen when I talk to you. Now take your own advice and count the strides between each jump. I have spaced them for six. Make sure she is jumping straight. If you get lazy, your horse will feel it immediately."

"Okay." DJ returned to a two-point trot, circled the ring, and cantered toward the first jump again. This time they flew over each obstacle without a pause. She didn't need Bridget to tell her she'd done a good job.

DJ and Joe were the last to arrive for dinner. As they walked in the door, two torpedoes hurled themselves against DJ's legs and clung. Two matching round faces with laughing blue eyes and smiles from dimple to dimple kept their mouths in perpetual motion.

"We been waiting for you. Where you been? How come you didn't come sooner? We comed to see you. Did you bring your horse?"

DJ looked from one to the other, doing her best to tell them apart. No such luck. "Okay, B & B, let me put my stuff down—"

"B & B!" The two shrieked in unison.

"Me's Billy, him's Bobby." The one on the right let go long enough to point.

"Well, how am I supposed to tell who's who?" DJ let a laughing Joe take her bag.

"The same way the rest of us do. We yell 'hey, you' and they both come." Joe grabbed one of the two and, with the giggling body clamped under his arm, headed for the kitchen. The other let loose DJ's leg and pelted after them.

DJ sucked in a deep breath. It was as if those two drained the room of oxygen. She started for the stairs when her gaze snagged on the two people standing by the French doors to the deck. Her five-feet-five mother looked tiny beside a taller and younger version of Joe Crowder. Robert's fair hair and great smile made him look like a movie star. DJ squinted; a tall and blond Tom Cruise filled the doorway. Her mother was laughing, her long earrings catching the light when she shook her head. She wore her hair pulled back on the sides, and, as usual, her clothes looked as if she'd just stepped out of a Nordstrom's window.

DJ looked down at her dirty jeans, a tear in one knee, her T-shirt liberally decorated with horse hairs. She could hear Gran with Joe and the twins in the kitchen. Everyone had someone but her.

Feeling both grungy and unneeded, she made her way up the stairs to take a shower.

"Dinner in fifteen minutes," Gran called after her.

DJ started to take her usual place at the table, but World War III erupted over the chair next to her.

"Me sit by DJ!"

"No." Big shove. "Me!"

"Hey, guys, we can fix this easy. I'll sit here." DJ pulled out the next chair over. "And then there's room on each side." Guess she was needed after all. They reached for her hands when Joe bowed his head for grace. "Thank you, Father, for this new family you have created. Thank you for the food that Melanie has so lovingly prepared. May we all seek to do your will. Amen."

Everyone joined in the amen. DJ glanced from one side of her to the other. The boys were two peas in a pod. When they grinned up at her, she felt her heart flutter and expand. She finally had cousins. And they were pretty cute.

But by the time she cut up their meat, helped pour milk, and answered fifty nonstop questions, she was wiped out. Robert was laughing at her across the table.

"Just tell 'em to knock it off." He put on a stern face. "Okay, guys, DJ would like to eat her dinner, too, you know."

"'Kay. *Then* will you show us your pictures?"

"Your horse pictures—the ones you drawed." The left side piped up. "Gran said you has lots of pictures."

"We draw pictures, too."

By the time dinner was over, DJ felt as though she'd just spent three hours at a tennis match. While the adults cleaned up, she took the boys upstairs to her room, where they oohed and aahed over her drawings.

"How about a story?" She took them with her to her bookshelf where she'd kept all her favorite books since she was a little girl. "You like Dr. Seuss?" At their enthusiastic agreement, she pulled *Cat in the Hat* off the shelf. She plumped her pillows into a stack, then snuggled against them, one boy tucked under each arm.

When they goodbyed Robert and the boys out the door, Robert leaned over to whisper in her ear. "They think you're better than Saturday morning cartoons, and that's really saying something."

"Thanks, I guess. I like them, too."

Robert said good-night to Lindy last. "I'll call you."

"Okay. You guys take care."

DJ watched from her spot by Gran and Joe. If she didn't know better, those were sappy looks her mother and Robert were sharing. The kind of look that lasts forever in the movies. Surely she was reading more into this than she saw.

She looked at Gran and recognized a misty look in her eyes, too. For pete's sake, what was going on here? If romance was contagious, she'd better look out.

"We better get going, too." Joe stepped back, taking Gran with him. "I have to be at the station at seven. Only thirteen more days to go, and I'll be a free man."

"And I have homework." DJ wished she could ask Gran to stay. Couldn't Joe get along without her once in a while?

"Me too." Lindy gave her mother a hug. "Thank you both for coming to our rescue again." When she hugged Joe, she whispered something into his ear.

The grin that split his face told DJ it was a compliment of some kind. "Me too," was all he said.

When the good-nights and goodbyes were all said and the door closed, DJ headed for her room. She had a paper to write on a book she'd read during the summer. At the moment, not one title came to mind. This hadn't been a summer with much time for reading.

When she studied her bookshelf, the only thing that caught her attention was the *American Pony Club Manual*. It was definitely American, though she doubted her teacher would call it great literature. She'd been studying that for the last three years.

She pulled it off the shelf, grabbed a piece of paper

out of her drawer, and started writing. She wrote fast, covering three pages before she realized it. After reading, rewriting, and copying, she stuck it in her folder. It would have to do.

Their last pony party on Saturday was a breeze compared to some of the others. Only four little kids, mothers who paid attention, and a hostess who gave them a bonus.

"That's my kind of party," DJ said when they trotted up the street on the way back to the Academy. "Makes me think we should continue."

"Think again. We said the end of summer was it. And summer's definitely over."

"I know, but where else could we have made this kind of money doing something we really like?"

Amy stopped and stared at her, shaking her head. "*We* really like pony parties? *We?* Dream on."

"Come on, you gotta admit we had fun—most of the time."

"Okay, I'll go along with that, but we just don't have time to do this. You said if you didn't keep your grades up, you'd have to quit working at the Academy. My dad said the same."

"You think they've been talking behind our backs?"

"They don't need to. Comes with the territory. And don't change the subject. We are *not* doing more parties."

"Until next summer," DJ muttered the words fast.

"Dream on."

"After I pay for Major, I won't even have two hundred dollars left, and I need a good jumping saddle."

"You can use one of the Academy's."

"Good thing, too. Saddles cost so much. How do those riders on the equestrian team manage? Going for the Olympics must cost a bundle."

"You're just figuring that out? That's why so many riders get sponsors."

They trotted Bandit up to his stall and unloaded their gear. All the while DJ's hands were busy with grooming the pony and putting him away, her mind turned over ideas of how to make money for her dream. She needed thousands and thousands of dollars, not just hundreds. She could barely imagine how she would come up with a hundred dollars, let alone thousands.

12

DJ FELT AS IF SHE WERE TRAPPED in a revolving door. Whenever she tried to jump out, it spun faster. Get up, go to school, study, come home, work at the Academy, come home, eat, study, fall into bed, and start all over again. The days that her mother did the cooking gave her a few extra minutes to memorize Latin conjugations.

Only the thought that she was banking hours at the Academy to pay for Major's keep kept her going. Was the entire year going to be like this?

Two days after Joe retired, they trailered Major out to the Academy. When the big horse stepped out of the trailer and looked around as if he owned the place, DJ had to fight the burning in her eyes. Major was hers—as soon as she paid her money, of course. At long last, she owned a horse. A good horse, too, better than she dreamed possible.

She sent a thank-you heavenward and backed Major the rest of the way down the ramp. "Such a good fella. How perfect can you be?"

"He's going to like it here." Joe's eyes looked suspiciously liquid. "Your having him couldn't make me happier."

Major lifted his head and let out a whinny that set DJ's ears ringing. Horses answered him from in the barn and the outside stalls.

"If you'll hold him, I'll go get a saddle. Bridget said to let her know when we got here so she could watch me ride him the first time." DJ handed Joe the lead shank. She'd fit her new bridle later.

While she gathered her tack, she could barely keep from yelling. Instead she whispered, "I have a horse. Major is mine. I'm riding *my* horse for the first time." She felt like tap-dancing through the air.

When she saddled Major, she was instantly grateful for her five-feet, seven-inch height. If she'd been a peanut like Amy, she'd have had to stand on a box to put the saddle in place.

She had to let the headstall out to the last notch to fit, but when everything was finally adjusted, she laid a hand over her heart to still its runaway pace.

"Can I give you a leg up?" Joe held the reins with one hand and cupped the other on his knee.

"Sure." Once in the saddle, she checked her stirrups, shortened one a notch, and checked again. This time when she straightened her legs, she felt balanced. And a long way from the ground. She looked down into the face of the man smiling up at her. "Thanks, Joe." She looked deep into his blue eyes, seeing nothing but love and pride shining there. "I have a question." At his nod, she continued. "Do you want to be called Gramps, Grandpa, or Joe?"

He blinked quickly, then cleared his throat. "Do you have a preference?"

"Well, since I'm DJ, you could be GJ—you know, Grandpa Joe."

"Could be." His chuckle invited a like response.

"But I think I'd rather call you Grandpa. I haven't had one of those for a long time, and my other one was pretty special."

"I'm sure he was. I'm honored to be your grandpa." Major gave him a nudge in the back. "I think our boy here is ready to do more than stand and listen to us talk." He turned and walked with them to the arena. "I'll get the gate."

Major moved out in a powerful, ground-eating walk. His smooth, even stride made DJ think about Patches and his spine-pounding hammer step. What a difference training made!

He responded to her aids almost before her thoughts became acts. Two-point trot, posting trot, canter. All controlled and as smooth as floating on a pool. What would he be like over a jump?

Reverse, figure eights, lead changes—he danced down the length of the arena as though they were performing to music. When she signaled him to back up, he did. Going sideways was no problem, either. She was almost afraid to move, in case this was all a dream and she might wake up in bed.

The sound of clapping brought her back to the real world. Bridget, Joe, Amy, Amy's father, and several others lined the aluminum rails.

"Do you bow, too?" Major flicked his ears back and forth at the sound of her voice.

DJ stopped him directly in front of Joe and Bridget. "He knows so much more than I do that it scares me. What if I'm not good enough for him?"

"Then he'll just make you better." Bridget studied the horse's head. "He has the look of a gentleman about him."

"You wouldn't say that if you were causing a disturbance and Major here figured it was his job to convince you differently. He's better than a German Shepherd for intimidating suspects."

"I'll remember that when my students get out of control."

DJ only half listened to them. She stroked Major's neck, reliving the experience she'd just had. Riding Major was like a piece of heaven—her own special piece.

"He's amazing," Amy said reverently.

"The two of you will definitely cause a sensation in the ring," Bridget said. "You look like you were made for each other."

"And to think he's spent all these years wasting away on the San Francisco police force." Joe winked at DJ.

"Those were his working years; now he gets to have fun." DJ motioned for Amy to open the gate. "Come on, I'll let you help me brush him down."

"You'll *let* me? How come I'm so honored?"

"You're my best friend, that's why." They headed for the barn, Amy trotting alongside.

"Does he feel as smooth as he looks?"

"Yup. You can ride him tomorrow if you like." DJ kicked her feet free of the iron stirrups and leaped to the ground. She stroked Major's neck and shoulder, running her hands over him as if memorizing every inch. When she led him to his stall, floored with fresh shavings, he looked around, acquainting himself with his new home. The horse in the stall next to him raised his nose to sniff through the bars. Major ignored him, snuffling the shavings, the hay rack, the full water bucket.

"You can have a drink as soon as we're finished."

Major raised his head, nickered at a horse that whin-nied to him, then stood perfectly still for DJ to remove his tack. After she replaced his bridle with a nylon web halter and turned him loose, he drank a couple swallows and again checked out his new quarters.

DJ watched his every movement as if she'd never seen a horse before.

Amy watched both the horse and her friend. "I think you're in love."

"I think you're right. I've been waiting for this day for fourteen years."

"Come on, you didn't want a horse the day you were born."

"How do you know? Maybe I did." DJ gave Major a final pat and closed the door behind her. "You gotta ad-mit it's been a long time."

When they got home, DJ went up to her room and opened her money box. Her bank account was now nearly empty. She lifted out the $380 they'd agreed upon and counted it again. Downstairs, she handed it to Joe.

"I don't know how to say enough thank-you's."

"You don't have to. I got the thrill of my life just watching you with him. And this way, I never have to tell him goodbye." He put the money in his billfold and drew out a folded piece of paper.

"Here's the bill of sale. We need to make this official, so after I sign it, you do the same. Then I'll make a copy for me. You get to keep this one. How's that?"

"Fine." Two thrills chased each other up and down her spine.

They both signed on the dotted lines. Joe reached out, and they shook hands.

"He's all yours." Joe, still holding her hand, patted it with his other. "With both mine and God's blessing."

DJ couldn't think of anything to say. But then, she would have had a hard time talking anyway.

The next afternoon when her students arrived, DJ stopped them before they could saddle their horses. "I have someone for you to meet."

"You got your horse!" Angie clapped her hands.

"Let's see." They grabbed DJ by the hands and dragged her down the aisle. She stopped in front of Major's stall. "Angie, Krissie, and Samantha, I'd like you to meet Major. Major, these horse-crazy girls are my students. You'll be going up in Briones with them some Saturday, so you might as well get to know them." Major arched his neck over the door and let each one of them pat his cheek.

"Wow! He's huge." "He's handsome." "I'm glad for you." The girls all spoke at the same time.

"Okay, back to work. I just had to show him off." DJ shooed them back to their stalls. She gave Major one last pat and followed them. His soft nicker followed her down the aisle.

"He already likes you," Angie said, picking up her saddle.

"Well, the feeling is sure mutual."

Now besides teaching, training Patches, and her other chores, she had to work Major. Had to, as in she'd die if she didn't. Within a week they were working him over the low jumps. He cleared them as though they were a waste of his time.

"Bit of a snob, is he?" Bridget said with a laugh one day.

DJ patted Major's sweaty neck. "He wants to go for the big ones. Like me."

"As soon as you both keep your timing consistent on these, we will talk about bigger jumps. Remember to count your strides between the jumps. You have to get that down to pure reflex. Timing is everything."

DJ nodded. She clamped her bottom lip between her teeth. She hated to have to be reminded of something so simple. But when they were jumping, she forgot everything but the glorious feel of it. She practiced as long as she dared before rushing home.

If this was life in the fast lane, she was keeping up— barely. But she wouldn't trade places with anyone for anything.

One afternoon there was a message from Gran on the machine when she got home from school. "I've called your mother at work and she says yes, so you have to come along. We'll pick you up at 7:00. I'm afraid you won't be able to spend all evening with Major. No jeans!" There was a pause, a giggle, and then her voice again. "And by the way, this includes dinner, so don't eat." DJ punched the rewind button and listened again. The message still didn't make a whole lot of sense.

She changed clothes and headed for the Academy. Since she had her students today, she'd hardly get any time for Major. As soon as she got to the Academy, she put him out on the hot walker to loosen him up.

Patches loosened her up. He tried to loosen her clear

off, but DJ had learned to read him and his tricks and was ready for him. He didn't like backing up. Not one bit.

"I know you like to be able to see where you're going, but you just have to learn to trust your rider. It's not as if I'm taking you into quicksand." His ears twitched back and forth as he listened to her. When she finished, he snorted and pawed the ground with one front foot. "Stop that!" Her sharp command caught his attention—fast.

This time he backed hesitantly. At least his ears were up. "Maybe that's what I need to do—yell at you."

"Mrs. Johnson started class with him today, but it did not go very well. Next time I am going to suggest she use one of the school horses until you have Patches better trained. I do not know why someone would go out and buy a green-broke horse for their child, especially for a boy like Andrew." Bridget shook her head. "Makes no sense to me."

DJ fought against the urge to hustle her class along. Every time she looked at her watch, it seemed the hands were racing to reach seven.

By the time she'd worked Major through the flat work, there was no time for jumping. What did Gran want that was so important anyway? Couldn't they do it on Saturday?

Everyone else was ready when she hit the door at 6:55. She held up a hand. "Don't panic, I'll make it." Four minutes and thirty seconds later, she shut the door on her room so her mother wouldn't see the mess. But she was ready. She could rebraid her hair in the car.

"Mother, what in the world is the big secret?" Lindy

leaned forward. She and DJ occupied the backseat of Joe's new Ford Explorer.

"This is the first time we've ridden in this car." DJ sniffed in the new-car fragrance. "It almost smells as good as Major."

"DJ!" Lindy's tone had that impatient parent sound.

"I'll take that as a compliment." Joe beamed at her in the rearview mirror.

"You just have to wait." Gran turned in her bucket seat. "In fact, you have to close your eyes. No peeking!"

DJ and Lindy both groaned, but did as they were told.

A few minutes later, the car stopped, and Gran said, "Open your eyes now."

DJ looked around. "This is your new house!"

"Mother . . . does this mean. . . ?"

"Yes. It's ours!" Gran dangled the keys with one hand and clasped Joe's with the other. "We're moving this weekend."

"Can we see it?" DJ shoved the car door open as she spoke.

"That's what we're here for. Robert will be here any minute with the boys. Sonja couldn't come today, but she and Andy will be here to help on Saturday." Gran led them on a grand tour as if they'd never seen a house before. DJ lingered in the room designated as hers. There was another guest room for the rest of the kids.

When the boys showed up, they each grabbed one of DJ's hands and made like they were stuck on with Crazy Glue. She could have used some glue on their mouths. Did little kids always ask this many questions?

On Saturday, as soon as she finished her work at the Academy, DJ rode her bike to Gran and Joe's new house, rather than riding home. It wasn't any farther and there weren't any hills on the way.

Sonja grinned a greeting and handed DJ a box. "Master bedroom. You and I can start on the kitchen next."

"Where's my mom?"

"She and Robert are at your house packing Melanie's bedroom things. They're going to use that set for your room."

"Oh." DJ thought of the room that had always been Gran's. It would now be empty. And all her things would be gone from the studio, too. An ache started in her middle and traveled to her eyes. She almost stumbled on the front step because she was blinking and rolling her eyes upward to keep the tears from falling. One more chunk was disappearing out of her life.

By the time they finished moving and devouring the pizzas Joe had ordered, the twins were sound asleep on the floor. DJ felt like joining them. She'd never moved in her life, and now she knew why. Moving was the pits.

"Oh, my aching back." Sonja lay flat on the carpet. "Wake me when Monday comes."

Gran rested her head on Joe's shoulder. "Thank you all so much. I don't know what we'd have done without you."

"Called a moving company," Andy, Joe's youngest son, said.

"How about having a housewarming next weekend at the same time as Joe's retirement party?" Gran sat up straight, her eyes catching a sparkle again at the thought of a party.

Groans met her suggestion.

"We'll have it catered. I know someone really good and not too expensive."

"You'd hire a caterer?" DJ jerked totally awake.

"Mother?" Lindy and DJ wore the same shocked expressions.

"You always do everything yourself," Lindy added.

"I know, but I'll probably still be busy putting things away, and with DJ's horse show the week after that, this weekend is our best option."

DJ scooted back to prop herself against Gran's legs. "You'd plan a housewarming around my horse show?"

"Darlin', of course. I can't miss that."

"That's not all. I'll be coming, too. She can't have a retirement party without the retiree there." Joe tweaked DJ's braid. "And I wouldn't miss your horse shows for the world."

DJ felt love wrap itself around her, snuggling into all the cracks and hollows. "Thanks, Grandpa." She reached over her shoulder to take Gran's hand and tilted her head back to wink up at the man on the seat above her. "You know, I think I like GJ better. Then our names nearly match. You now, DJ and GJ. What do you think?"

"I think anything you call me is fine." He cleared his throat in the middle of the sentence.

"Well, we better get going so we can come back tomorrow and help some more." Lindy started to rise and Robert leaped to his feet to pull her upright.

"Your car isn't here. How about if I give you and DJ a ride home?"

"Thanks." Lindy started picking up the leftover trash from the pizza. "Oh, did I tell you?" She stopped in front of the couch where Gran and Joe sat. "There may be a new position opening up in L.A. My boss thinks it's ideal for me, or I'm ideal for it."

Only a huff in the breathing of one of the twins broke the absolute silence.

DJ couldn't breathe. An invisible elephant was squashing her like a bug.

13

WAS HER MOTHER TOTALLY off-the-wall bonkers?

"Thanks for the ride," Lindy said when they arrived home. She prodded DJ.

"Yeah, thanks."

"See you tomorrow?" DJ heard Robert ask, but she didn't wait for her mother's answer. If she never in her whole life spoke to her mother again, it would be too soon. She didn't stomp. She didn't yell. She didn't cry. She unlocked the front door, left it open for her mother, and walked up the stairs to her room. This door she shut. The click sounded loud in the silence.

She crossed the room and stood in front of the window. It was a good thing breathing didn't take thought and effort, because she wouldn't have bothered. How could she ever afford to keep Major in Los Angeles? How would she find a stable? She knew Bridget gave her extra help without charging. Would anyone else do that? And Amy. How could she leave Amy? And Gran and Joe? She couldn't live without Gran.

Gran. The thought stopped the panic like throwing a light switch.

"DJ?" Her mother knocked at the bedroom door. "DJ, I want to talk with you."

DJ crossed the room and opened the door. She stood right in the doorway, making it very obvious that her mother wasn't welcome.

"DJ, don't panic yet. Nothing has been decided. I just wanted to give you time to think about it."

"Doesn't matter. You do what you want. I'll go live with Joe and Gran." DJ crossed her arms over her chest. She met her mother's shocked gaze with a perfectly blank face.

"But, it will be a better job, more money, more . . ." Lindy took a step backward. "We'll discuss this when I know more about the job."

"Fine." DJ could feel one eyebrow twitch as if it wanted to form a question mark of its own. "Good-night, Mother." She stepped back and quietly shut the door.

DJ didn't know she could do it—not talk to her mother, that is. Usually she did everything but stand on her head to get back in her mother's good graces. This time she didn't care. She wasn't the one who had decided to move to L.A., no matter what her daughter wanted and needed. *Grown-ups are good at that*, DJ thought. *Always so sure they know best. They don't always—unless they're like Gran and Joe.* "I will *not* give up my dream," DJ promised the face in the bathroom mirror. "I *will* ride in the Olympics someday." She tugged the brush through her hair. "And I will *not* give up Major."

Monday her art teacher announced an art contest for local students. "The entry can be in any medium: pen and ink, charcoal, water colors, tempera, oils, or acrylics. The choice of subject is your own, and you can enter a class project or one you've done at home. Just don't use any outside help."

Mentally DJ flipped through the horses she'd done. She could think of a flaw in every one. It would have to be something new, but she would stick with pen and ink or pencil. She brought her mind back to her classwork with difficulty. She'd much rather start the drawing now.

"Can I see a show of hands of those who think they'll enter?"

DJ's hand was the first in the air.

That evening, as soon as she finished all her home chores after the hours at the Academy, she took out her pad and pencils. She closed her eyes. She could just see Major clearing the triple. She started to draw.

It seemed like only a few minutes had passed, but her scratchy eyes and the nearly complete picture told her otherwise. She glanced at the clock. Midnight. Had she heard her mother come up to bed? Vaguely she remembered a knock at the door and her mother's voice bidding her to sleep well. She fell into bed, asleep before she could pull up the covers.

A noise jerked her out of a sleep so deep she hadn't heard the birds serenade her with their morning song. A car horn. She checked her clock. Seven-thirty! What had happened to her alarm? As she bailed out of bed, she couldn't remember setting the stupid thing. She ran to a window in her mother's bedroom and called down to Amy.

"I just woke up. Can you give me five minutes?"

Mr. Yamamoto waved and nodded.

DJ threw on her clothes, brushed her teeth, gathered

her hairbrush and bands, grabbed her backpack, and raced down the stairs. No time for breakfast. She dumped the box of food bars over the counter in her rush to get one.

She felt as though she were an hour behind all day. She dragged from lack of sleep. Still rushing when she got home from school, she fixed a sandwich, grabbed a juice package, and pedaled as fast as she could to the Academy, eating as she rode. When she did think of the mess she'd left behind, she promised herself to get home early to clean it before her mother got there.

She made herself calm down once she reached the Academy. The more you rushed a horse, the longer it took to accomplish anything.

Major greeted her with a nicker, nosing her pockets for the treats she always carried. DJ could tell Joe had been there. The stall was clean, horse groomed, and a note pinned to the outer wall.

See you later. I rode Major this morning, so he's already had some exercise. Bridget found me a Quarter Horse to look at. Want to come along? GJ.

DJ read the note again. Of course she wanted to go along, but when? Major reached out to take a taste of the paper. "What are you, half goat? You can't eat everything! Stop that." She yanked it away, but not before he took a sizable nibble out of one corner.

DJ opened the stall door and, with a hand on his nose, backed him up. She turned and stood with his head over her shoulder, rubbing his ears and his face. He sighed and tipped his head a bit so she could reach another spot.

She could hear people talking in another part of the barn and horses moving around in their stalls, but here, for this moment, she felt peace. It was easy to forget that her mother was considering moving to L.A., that they didn't get along, that she had enough to do to keep three people busy. She turned her face to sniff the best fragrance in the world—horse.

The good feeling remained until she got home. The garage door was open. Gran's minivan wasn't there, so that meant only one thing. Right now she prayed it was burglars. But no such luck. Her mother had come home early.

DJ quietly put her bike away, closed the garage door, and opened the door to the kitchen. Going into the house was like stepping into a meat locker set on deep freeze.

No more mess on the counter. DJ chewed her lip. Her mother had been home awhile. She listened, holding her breath to hear better. Sounds came from upstairs. Water running. She tried to remember. Had she closed her bedroom door? The bathroom was a disaster too.

"Well, you better get it over with." She dredged up every available bit of courage and climbed the stairs. "Please, God, don't let her ground me again. I don't have time for that right now. What with the show coming and all."

Lindy turned from scrubbing the sink in the bathroom. The counter was neat, the dirty towels in the hamper, and new ones on the racks. The scene registered in DJ's mind at the same time as the scowl on her mother's face. Compared to here, the kitchen had been balmy.

"I . . . I'm sorry. I overslept and—"

"Darla Jean, if you are that tired, then it's time we made some changes around here—"

"No, I just forgot to set my alarm."

"Forgot? Or was too tired?" Lindy gave the sink one last wipe and flicked off the light. She pointed the way to her daughter's room. "Your bedroom looks like a tornado went through there."

"I know."

"Your light was still on at 11:30 last night. Homework?"

"Well . . ." DJ tried to think whether she could call her art project homework.

"You've got too much to do—"

"Yeah, taking care of the house and yard besides school and my work at the Academy *is* hard."

"Are you saying I don't do anything around here?"

"No—well, yes." DJ threw up her hands. "You're never home. Why do you care?"

"That would be one of the good things about the job in L.A. I'd be home more, do less traveling."

"Goody for you. I don't care if you are home. I didn't mean to leave a mess, and I would have cleaned it up. I always do. You don't care about me and what I like at all. You never have." DJ caught herself. She'd used always and never after promising that when she had kids, she wouldn't use it.

"Go to your room, Darla Jean, I just can't deal with any more of this right now."

"Gladly." DJ spun around and left as ordered. At least she hadn't been grounded—yet.

She threw herself across her unmade bed. Why couldn't she and her mother talk without yelling at each other? It wasn't as though she'd murdered someone or stolen the family jewels. She just hadn't gotten all her chores done. And the day wasn't even over yet. If her mother had come home when she usually did, everything would have been fine. *I shoulda run away when I had the chance.* Her stomach rumbled. You'd think her mother would spend the time to make a meal for her daughter, rather than clean up a mess that wasn't that bad to start with. But no good smells came from the kitchen, unless you liked the smell of polish and disinfectant.

She got up and started putting away her clothes. After making the bed and cleaning off her desk, she picked up the horse drawing she'd been working on last night. It was good, the best she'd done. Now if Gran were here, she'd take the picture to her and they'd discuss the quality of lines, the perspective, the balance of the horse. If only Gran were here.

Maybe she should pray her mother got that stupid job in L.A. so she could live with Gran and Joe. She propped the picture on the top of her chest of drawers and stepped back. Another thought hit her: What if Gran and Joe wouldn't let her live with them? What if they didn't want any kids around? What would happen to her and Major then?

14

"OVER MY DEAD BODY."

"But, M-o-m." DJ immediately erased any trace of whine. This time she would present her idea just as she and Amy had their pony club plan. Businesslike and to the point.

"Mother, please listen to me. I've come up with a way to get more done in my day, and I'd like us to talk about it." She hesitated a moment. "Please?" She kept her hands behind her back so her crossed fingers didn't show.

Lindy started to say something, then changed her mind. "All right. Since you've put so much thought into this, I'll listen. But that doesn't mean I have to agree."

Two days had passed since their last blowup. Nothing more had been said, so DJ knew she would not be grounded. But this morning she had woken up with a gonzo idea. Amy agreed with her. Amy also advised her on how to handle her mother. Now they'd see if this new approach worked.

DJ took a deep breath and made sure she had a pleasant expression on her face. "Mom, you've always told me that it is important to have goals and work toward them."

"Of course." Lindy turned her head a fraction to the side. Her look said, what's up?

"Like you do. You know my goal is to ride in the Olympics one day." Lindy nodded. She leaned back against the sofa and crossed her arms.

"So."

"So, most of the Olympic contenders, like the ice skaters and the gymnasts, work out for a couple of hours before school, then again afterward. I never—" she caught herself. She had just overslept. "I *like* getting up early. Morning's a good time for me. If I could work with Major at about six or so, then I'd have more time in the evening for stuff around here."

Lindy was shaking her head already. "You're not riding up to the Academy in the dark. That road is too dangerous."

"You could drop me off on your way to work."

"How would you get home to get ready for school?"

"I could take my clothes and have Mr. Yamamoto pick me up there. I don't think he'd mind."

"Oh, sure. You'd go to school smelling like horse." She made "horse" sound like a dirty word.

DJ bit her tongue just in time. One smart remark would ruin everything. So her mother didn't think horses smelled good. So what? Not everyone had to love horses like DJ.

"Please, just think about it?" DJ clamped her fingers together, hard. *Please, God, make her change her mind.*

DJ now knew what a bug under a microscope must feel like. The look her mother was giving her seemed to see right through her. She'd done her best. Now it was time to wait.

The silence seemed to stretched from then till Christmas.

Was that a smile breaking through? The corners of her mother's mouth had twitched.

"All right, I'll think about it." Lindy held up a hand to stop DJ before she spun into orbit. "I only agreed to think about it. Now you have to agree not to bug me for a decision. I'll tell you when I'm ready."

DJ nodded. That wasn't the answer she wanted, but it sure beat "over my dead body." And they'd managed to talk about something really important without fighting. She should put a star on the calendar.

Lindy still hadn't made a decision by Saturday. DJ now had one week to finish preparing Major for their first show. And today was Gran and Joe's open house. She'd quit thinking about her mother moving to Los Angeles. No news was good news. She had enough else on her mind.

"I'm going right over to Gran's from the Academy," she called to her mother through the closed bedroom door. All she got in response was an "humphf," but she knew her mother had heard.

"Did you finish your drawing for the contest?" Amy asked on their trek to the Academy.

"Almost. I still have some shading to do. I was going to show it to Gran, but she's been so busy getting ready for the party, I thought I'd work some more and then see what she says. So far, it's the best I've ever done—at least

I think so." Yelling and pedaling at the same time took all her breath.

They halted at the stop sign and looked back over their shoulders. The sun, with only a rim up over the horizon, painted the scattered clouds in shades of pink and rose with lavender tops.

"Wish I had my camera."

"You always think of that too late."

"I know, I should carry it all the time. Hey, did I tell you my idea?"

DJ raised an eyebrow.

"I'm going to take pictures of the party today and put them in an album as my wedding present to Joe and Gran. What do you think?"

"Fantastic, she'll love it. We could make little labels with funny sayings and stick them underneath."

"Perfect. See you at the party."

DJ got to the party by a different mode of transportation. She rode Bandit, who would be the entertainment for the younger set. She managed to get there, take a shower, and dress before the party began.

"Here, darlin', please put these platters on the table."

"Sure. I thought you were having this catered." DJ picked up the round tray of vegetables and dip.

"I did. I bought all these, but I couldn't see any sense in having someone else do the serving."

"That's what we have kids for." Joe took two platters.

"And grandkids." Shawna returned from arranging the napkins.

Robert and Lindy arrived together, along with the twins.

DJ caught her raising eyebrow. Her mother hadn't

said she wasn't bringing the car. The thought got buried under the twins' onslaught.

"You brought a pony! What's his name? Can we ride now? I'm first. No, me!"

"Boys, boys." Robert shrugged his apology. "What can I say, DJ? They like you."

DJ peeled them off her legs. "All right, let's go. Shawna, you coming?"

Andy and Sonja were setting up the volleyball net when DJ got dragged out to the yard by the two B's.

"Hey, we can use some more hands." Andy waved to them.

"No, we's riding!" one of the B's informed him.

"Ex-cu-se me."

DJ stopped them before they reached the pony. "You can only ride on one condition."

"What?" They tugged on her hands.

"When I say you're done, you have to get off. No arguments. Understood?" She used the tone of voice that worked best with her students.

They started to frown, then changed their minds and flashed their sunniest smiles. *How'd they do that?* DJ wondered. *They do things at the same time without ever talking about it.* "Now remember, a horse can't see behind him, so when you come up, talk to him, let him know you're there." She suited her acts to her words. "Hey, Bandit, ready to give these guys a ride?" While she talked, she retightened the saddle girth, then untied him and put his bridle back on over his halter. "Sorry, fella, you can eat more later."

She turned to the boys. "Okay, first time around you ride together; then one at a time."

Even though the rides went well, by the time DJ had

given every little kid there a turn, she was dragging her wagon.

"I could lead for a while, if you'd like," Shawna suggested softly. "You can go get something to eat."

"I better not leave him. If something happened, it would be my fault."

"Then tie him up and come join the rest of the party." Robert appeared at her side. "Even though you're family, you don't have to be slave labor."

DJ took him at his word. She tied up Bandit, warned the kids to stay away from him, and went in to feed her rumbling stomach. After eating, yakking with Amy, and shooshing Gran out of the kitchen, she wandered out to the backyard where she could hear shouts from the family caught up in a wild volleyball game.

"Come on, DJ, you can be on my team." Robert waved at her.

"No, she can't. Lindy's on your team." Sonja grabbed the bottom of the net, toe to toe with her brother-in-law.

"Lot of good that does." Lindy wiped her brow with the back of her hand. "Athletic, I'm not."

"Robert doesn't care," Andy yelled from the back row of his team. "Come on, DJ. We'll pound 'em into the dirt."

DJ did as they said, but the shock of seeing grass stains on her mother's knees and the seat of her white shorts was too much. *Her* mother, Lindy Randall, playing volleyball?

When it was DJ's turn to serve, she stepped behind the line and drilled an overhand serve right at her mother.

Lindy squealed and ducked. The ball hit her shoulder and went out of bounds. "Not fair."

"Good job, kid. Do it again." Andy clapped his hands and winked at her.

DJ looked straight at her mother. And served to Joe. He bumped it up and Robert spiked it over the net. DJ bumped it to Andy, who set it for her. Jumping up with all her might, DJ spiked the ball. Robert got under it, but the ball spun out of bounds.

"Yes!" DJ grabbed air with her fist and pumped down. Andy slapped her hands. Sonja threw her arms around DJ and jigged her in a circle. "You spiked one down on ol' Robert. You're great at this."

"How come you're not on the volleyball team at your school?" Andy asked. "You're a good player."

"No time. And I'd rather ride any day. But I love playing."

"Well, let's just run this play again. You ready, Robbie, old man?"

Their team won 15–5.

"Want to go again?" Sonja yelled.

"In your dreams." Joe leaned over, panting. "I think it's time I leave this game to the younger generation."

"Not on your life." Robert slapped his dad on the back. "You're going to have to do something to stay in shape now that you're off the force."

"Well, I'll tell you a secret, volleyball against those three dynamos isn't it."

"You two probably could have done better without me to fall over." Collapsed on the ground, Lindy wiped her face with her shirttail. She picked a grass blade out of her hair, then combed it back with her fingers.

"Nah, you were great." Gallant Robert sank down beside her.

"Daddy. Daddy!" The two B's charged across the

court to throw themselves on him. The three guys tumbled over in a giggling heap of arms and legs.

"Sorry, they couldn't sit still another minute." Gran followed them out of the house. "I thought for a few minutes they were going to take an *n-a-p*." She spelled the word.

DJ watched the boys roughhouse with their father. If she'd known her dad, would they have had times like this when she was little? She caught herself in surprise. How come all of a sudden she was thinking of him again—whoever he was?

"I made a fresh pot of coffee, and there's plenty of food left. Come on inside," Gran said.

Everyone lumbered to their feet, pulled the twins off their father, and headed for the house. Once they were all served and seated in the living room, Andy looked over at Lindy.

"So, you heard any more about that job in L.A.?"

DJ's gaze flew to her mother.

Lindy took a long time looking up from her plate. "I have an interview down there on Friday morning."

DJ choked on her bite of ham.

15

"GRAN, PLEASE, PLEASE, can I come live with you?"

Gran smoothed tendrils of hair back from DJ's forehead. "I don't know, darlin'. We'll just have to pray about it and see what God says. It might be that Lindy won't get that job."

DJ humphed. "Not hardly. You know how good she is. They'd be stupid not to hire her. Gran, I *can't* move away now. Everything I want is right here." DJ swallowed, bit her lip, blinked. Nothing was working out. One big fat tear slid down her cheek.

Gran gathered her close. The urge to rest her head on Gran's shoulder and cry until she ran out of tears made DJ pull away. She sniffed any other tears back and made herself stand up straight.

"My Bible verse won't work for this, Gran." DJ shook her head. "There's nothing I can do."

Gran stroked DJ's cheek with the gentle touch of love. "Then I have another one for you to think about. *Trust in the Lord with all your heart and lean not on your own understanding.*"

"You are awesome." DJ couldn't stop the tiny smile

that insisted on accompanying the words. "How do I do that?"

"Just tell Him you're trusting Him to work out this situation for the best for everybody."

"That's hard. I want what's best for *me*." DJ studied the cuticles on her hand. Only one was hanging in shreds. One fingernail had actually begun to grow. Her verse floated through her mind.

I can do all things through Christ who strengthens me. But she hadn't even been working on it—much. She stared at the fingernail. "God, I'm trusting you to work this out for the best for everyone." How come a whisper could hurt so?

"What's going on here?" Joe entered the kitchen, but stopped short when he saw DJ's face. He wrapped his arms around both Gran and DJ. "Don't worry, love. It'll all work out."

"I better get Bandit back to the Academy before dark." DJ stepped outside the hug. "I'm glad you're in your new house, and I had a good time at the party." She turned and fled out the back door as if a pack of wolves were on her heels.

Successful at outwitting the other kids, she trotted Bandit up the drive. Off to the left she saw her mother and Robert walking along the rail fence frosted with pink roses. They looked to be having a serious discussion.

"Tell her not to move," DJ muttered.

The empty house didn't seem so bad when she got home. She had a lot of serious thinking to do and the quiet helped. Not talking to her mother was getting easier and easier.

Monday she turned in her drawing. Gran had told her not to change anything when she saw it on Saturday. Tuesday her mother brought home pizza for dinner and insisted DJ eat with her.

"We have to talk." Lindy set out napkins and put the pizza box in the center of the table.

Go ahead and talk. There's no law that says I have to answer. DJ brought two cans of soda from the fridge and took her usual place.

"So, how are things going?"

"Fine."

"Are you ready for the show Saturday?"

DJ looked up from shoving strings of cheese into her mouth. *As if you cared.* She finished chewing and swallowed. "I guess."

"About Saturday . . ."

DJ felt like clapping her hands over her ears. "Listen, you do what you have to do, and I'll do what I have to do." She took another bite of pizza.

"No, *you* listen. I have an interview Friday. Gran has already said you can spend Thursday night there, and I'll be back Friday night. Robert and I will be attending your show."

"*You* are coming to my horse show?" DJ nearly choked on her pizza.

Lindy nodded. "With the boys."

"Oh great." *It was bad enough when Joe was coming, now the whole family was going to be there.* And she had thought the butterflies were bad before.

"Have you thought more about my taking the job down there?"

DJ looked at her as if she'd left her brains in her purse. *Had she thought about it?* Only repeating her

Bible verse kept her from going totally looney.

"You don't have to be sarcastic."

"I didn't say a word."

"You didn't have to."

Lindy tossed the tough end of the crust in the box. "I'm just trying to do what's best."

"I know."

Wednesday DJ let the jitters for the up-coming show get to her, and Major refused a jump. She calmed herself and him down and tried again. No problem.

"Come on, DJ, you know better than to let a show get to you." Bridget waited in the middle of the arena for DJ to complete another circuit.

"But this is the first time on my own horse. Not to mention entering a jumping event."

"I think it would be better if you did not enter the jumping event this first show. You and Major need to get more accustomed to each other first. See how you do." It was as though someone had turned off the sun. Bridget didn't think they were ready yet. She could enter anyway. But maybe this was for the best. "Can we leave this open to change if we're really doing well?"

"Of course. Is anything else bothering you?"

Oh, nothing. It's just that my mother might be leaving, and there'll be a big fight if I have to go along. That and we don't even talk to each other anymore. "No, I'm fine."

"I do not believe you." A smile took the sting out of the words. "Do not worry about this weekend. You will do fine."

Thursday night was the first time she stayed over at Joe and Gran's. Joe met her at the Academy and helped her give Major a bath. By the time they finished, the big horse shone as if they'd waxed him.

"You have time on Wednesday to go take a look at that cutting horse Bridget found?"

DJ thought a minute. "Sure. I don't teach that day."

"I know. That's why I chose it."

DJ leaned her forehead against Major's shoulder. Only two more days to go. One, actually, because they showed Saturday morning. Any time she swallowed, it seemed the swallow went only so far down before it twanged around like a ball on the end of a rubber string.

"DJ, can I help?" Joe spoke softly, all the while keeping his hands busy grooming Major.

"I wish. I just have to get through this first show." Her chuckle sounded hollow in the dimness. "I tell my students not to let the butterflies bother them, but look at me. I'm a basket case."

"I think it's more than just the show."

"I think you see too much." DJ retrieved her new show sheet from off the door and laid it over Major's back. Together she and Joe adjusted all the straps and buckles. "You stay clean now, Major. You gotta look your best on Saturday."

Friday she had a surprise quiz in Latin. It was a surprise all right. More like a shock actually. For the first five minutes her brain refused to function. *Please, God.* She shrugged her shoulders up to her ears, took a breath, and reread the first question.

She wrote fast and finished answering the questions just as the teacher called time. She handed in her paper with a sigh of relief. That was one way to take her mind off the weekend.

Joe picked her up at the Academy, and they drove to his house for dinner.

"You think butterflies are contagious?"

DJ looked at him, eyebrows questioning. "You're not the one entering."

"I know, but I think being a grandparent may be even worse in this case. I remember feeling this way when Robert played basketball. When he went to the free-throw line, I almost threw up."

"Come on, it wasn't that bad."

"Almost. You ask him sometime."

"Well, if you ever run out of butterflies, I'll gladly share some of mine."

"I've got good news and bad news," Gran said when they walked into the kitchen.

DJ started to shake her head. She knew what was coming.

"Lindy called."

"I knew it. She isn't coming home tonight and won't be at the show tomorrow. Now, what's the bad news?"

"The good news is you get to stay here again so I can make sure you get off all right in the morning."

"You're right, Gran. That part is good news."

"She said she'd come straight to the showgrounds. Robert and the boys are meeting her there."

"Great." *Maybe my events will be over by the time they get there.*

Having someone to help her in the morning gave DJ an extra boost. Joe joined forces with Mr. Yamamoto, and together with the other fathers, they had horses and riders loaded in record time.

"Now, all of you have your tack and riding gear?" Bridget stuck her head in each vehicle and asked the question. When everyone was ready, she waved to the driver in the first truck. "Let's go." The Academy parade had begun.

"Don't even think about it!" DJ gave herself such a stern order that Amy, who had tied Josh next to Major, turned to look at her.

"What are you mumbling about."

"Hunter/jumper."

"I thought Bridget told you not to enter that."

"She suggested it."

"Yeah, and Bridget only makes suggestions. Come on, there'll be another event in less than a month. Just wait."

"I've been waiting all my life."

"You know what I mean."

The loudspeaker crackled and a tinny voice echoed from the tree right above them. "First call for English Pleasure."

"Well, Major, old man, you and I better head for the warm-up ring." She unbuckled his halter, slipped it off his nose, and rebuckled it around his neck, just for safe keeping.

"You need some help?" Joe stopped right beside her. Major nickered, his nostrils barely moving. "I know, old son, it's time for you to earn your keep. Now you do everything DJ tells you, hear?"

DJ could have sworn the horse understood every word Joe said. She finished buckling the chin strap on the bridle and checked the reins.

"I hardly recognized you." Joe gave her a look full of approval.

"First time I've worn my new clothes. I got them for my birthday." DJ knew she looked good because she felt it. The black jacket, tan pants, and white stock looked put together and very professional.

"Between the two of you, you'll catch the judge's eye for sure."

"Good luck, DJ. Go get 'em." Her students wished her well.

"You can do it." Amy added her encouragement.

"Sure we can." DJ tried to smile but her mouth wobbled instead. "Come on, big fella, let's do it."

Joe walked with her on the dirt trail around the ring. "I have cloth in my back pocket," he told her. "To take care of all this dust."

DJ managed a smile, a small one, but a smile nevertheless. She looked over at the bleachers. Gran sat by herself. "If you want to go sit with Gran, you can. Major and I will be fine."

"I will, soon as you go in the ring."

DJ let him give her a leg up, checked her stirrup length, and smiled down at him. "Thanks, Joe, for all you've done."

"How's your stomach feeling now?"

"Better. When we enter that ring, I'll be having too much fun to think about butterflies." Just then a couple of them did flips and invited their friends to join them. DJ looked up in time to see Robert and the twins sit down beside Gran. How'd her butterflies know?

Major turned his head to nuzzle Joe's shoulder.

"Knock 'em dead, you two." Joe gave each of them a pat and crossed the dirt staging area to the log seats that made up the viewing stands.

DJ worked Major easily through his paces, letting him take his time while she exchanged remarks with other riders. She could feel herself relaxing. This was what she loved to do. Like actors loved the camera or the stage, she loved horse shows.

"English Pleasure to the ring. English Pleasure to the ring."

DJ trotted Major the remaining distance around the warm-up ring and out the gate. Joe stood there, cloth in hand. He wiped off Major's nose, legs, and hooves. With a soft brush, he ran quickly over the horse's rump. "Okay, now you really are ready."

DJ blew him a kiss. She entered the ring, third in line. Major acted as if he'd been showing all his life. Ears pricked forward, taking in everything around him, he did everything DJ asked. Walk, trot, canter, reverse. When she came too close to a rider in front, she turned him in a circle into the ring and back in line. He changed gaits smoothly and on command.

The judge motioned them into line in the center of the ring. The horse on their left refused to stand, and the rider had to take him out of line and bring him back. Twice.

Major never moved. The big horse could have been carved in granite.

The judge started with the lower ribbons, and the spectators gave each rider a burst of applause. When she handed DJ the blue, cheers and whistles broke out— mostly from the academy line-up.

DJ tried to be cool about the whole thing, but the smile she gave the judge for the ribbon and the sack of feed donated by a local feed store could have warmed Alaska.

"Congratulations. It's good to see you back in the ring."

"Thank you. This is his first time out." She patted Major's neck.

"Well, you certainly couldn't tell by that performance. Good luck with him."

DJ looked up to the stands. Her mother sat beside Robert, and she was clapping harder than anyone. Anyone but Joe, that is. When he met her at the gate, she could have sworn he'd had to wipe away moisture from his eyes—tears maybe?

DJ dismounted so they could walk together. After his congratulatory hug, he strolled beside her, letting the silence be. For a change DJ felt no need to fill the silence. "I'm really proud to own him, Joe. Thank you so much for making this part of my dream come true."

"I can see we're going to do a lot of dream building together, darlin'. You are a real pro."

The next class didn't go as well; DJ and Major only got a white.

"You were the best out there." Angie looked ready to take on the judge.

"You got ripped." Krissie was all ready to join her.

"Thanks for the vote of confidence, but the judge didn't see it that way. Being a good sport is a part of the game."

DJ's mind flitted back to the question she'd been asking herself all day. *Should I, or shouldn't I?* One minute she was all ready to register for the Hunter/Seat jumping class. The next she remembered what Bridget had said. But Major wasn't acting like a new trainee. He loved it out there.

She left the horse area and went to sit by her family.

"The boys are ready to start riding tomorrow." Robert kept them corralled, one under each arm. "Did you hear them hollering for you? If the judge hadn't given you a ribbon, they were ready to attack."

Bobby and Billy looked up at her, their faces serious for a change.

"Can I hold your ribbon?"

"Me too?" They didn't even yell.

Joe leaned closer. "I think it's your outfit. They aren't one-hundred percent sure it's really you in there."

DJ looked over at her mother, sitting on the other side of Gran. The two wore matching grins of pride. "Thanks for coming, Mom, Gran." To her own surprise, DJ realized she meant it. Having her mother here for the first time to see a horse show made the day even better. "I better get back to work. See you later."

Should she, or shouldn't she?

"What do you think, Ames?" The two of them spent the lull between entries leaning on the arena fence in front of the horse line.

"I think you should do what Bridget suggested." Amy made "suggested" sound like ordered. She raised an eyebrow when DJ groaned.

"DJ, come help me." The cry came from one of her students.

Sam's horse had kicked his neighbor.

DJ ran a hand down the kicked leg. She wiped away a dirt smudge. "He just grazed it. Let's put some more space be—no, let's move him to the end of the line." She assisted the transfer, and when she got back to the fence, she'd decided.

If one of her students went against her advice, she'd be peeved. What if Sam had said no to the move. DJ carefully hung her jacket on a hanger in the tack box. She placed her helmet in a plastic bag to keep it clean.

Amy gave her a thumbs-up sign.

"We'll jump another day," she whispered to Major's flicking ears. "By then we'll be so good, they'll beg us to jump." She tickled his whiskers and slipped him a horse cookie.

"Last call for novices on the lead. Hunter/Seat will follow."

DJ swallowed—hard. With one last look at the riders coming into the arena, she turned and headed down the line to see if Hilary needed any help.

"I'm fine, thanks. I was hoping you'd be in the ring with me." Hilary rechecked the girth on her saddle.

"So was I. Next time."

"Major looked really great out there. He was having fun, wasn't he?"

"Yep, me too."

"Everything all right here?" Bridget stopped beside them, her clipboard a natural extension of her arm.

"How come DJ's not entering Hunter/Seat?" Hilary asked.

"Do you want to?"

Dumb question. Did kids like ice cream? "B-but you said—"

"I said our discussion was open to change. You and Major have done a fine job. He appeared comfortable out there—in fact, I think he likes to show off, so I . . ." she glanced down at her list. "I entered the two of you. Joe is coming over to help you get ready. Any questions?"

DJ shook her head.

"Then what are you waiting for?" Bridget tapped DJ on the shoulder. "Don't rush—and concentrate."

"And count his strides." DJ touched her finger to her

forehead in a salute and dog-trotted back to where Joe was already saddling Major.

"I'll get my jacket." Her heart thundered in her throat. They were going to jump. Granted the jumps were low and easy, but this was it. Her first time.

Major was scheduled to jump last, but waiting didn't seem to bother him at all. "Remember, he's used to patrol. A lot of nothing goes on for hours. He learned years ago that getting excited only raises a sweat." Joe wiped the beads of moisture off his forehead. "Hot here today, isn't it?"

DJ looked at him to see if he realized what he'd said. His wink let her know he did. "You're the best, GJ."

"Give 'em a run for their money, DJ." He boosted her into the saddle. "See ya."

Major trotted into the arena, ears forward, seeming to float above the ground. He took the jumps like a veteran, never a hesitation, at a perfect pace. Each time he leaped into the air, DJ reminded herself to count.

The judge conferred with another when all the entrants had jumped. DJ and Hilary kept their horses at a standstill.

"For a first-timer, that was wonderful." Hilary gave DJ a smile to match her compliment.

"You'll get the blue, just watch." Even while DJ said what she felt to be true, she wished—oh, how she wished—for the blue.

Again the judge started at the lower end. She worked her way up, leaving Hilary, DJ, and one other rider for the three remaining ribbons.

"Number 43, a white ribbon goes to . . ."

DJ didn't hear the rider's name and horse. The blood pounded through her ears and out to her fingertips.

"The red goes to . . ." The judge paused. DJ couldn't find any spit to swallow.

"Number 61, DJ Randall on Major."

DJ pasted a smile on her face and trotted forward. She leaned over to accept the ribbon and thanked the judge.

"Hilary Jones, also of The Briones Riding Academy, earned the blue today, along with a halter donated by Pleasant Hill Feed Store."

DJ clapped along with the rest. "Next time, Major. You keep your eye on that ribbon because we want two blues next time." She leaned over to slap high fives with Hilary.

"I am very glad I was not the judge." Bridget met them when they left the arena. "You can both go home proud of what you accomplished."

That kind of compliment from Bridget was better than a ribbon any day.

By the end of the day, weary riders and fathers loaded weary horses. When they had all the animals back in their stalls and the tack put away, Joe reminded DJ that Robert was taking them all out for dinner.

"I'd rather go home." DJ didn't want to sound ungrateful, but beat didn't begin to describe the way she felt.

"We won't be late."

"Did Mom say anything about her trip?" Now that the excitement was over, reality crowded back in.

Joe shook his head.

"Where are we going?" DJ looked over at Joe when he turned into his own driveway.

"The boys voted for fried chicken." He winked at her. "It was supposed to be a surprise."

"I'm surprised."

When everyone had dished up their plates in the kitchen and found places to sit around the long dining-room table, DJ and her two shadows sat directly across from Robert and Lindy. *So what did they decide? To hire you on the spot? Have you already found a place to live?*

DJ kept her mouth under tight rein. Answering the boys' questions gave her no time to ask any of her own.

Robert clapped his hands for attention. "Lindy has something she'd like to say." Silence blanketed the table.

Lindy gave DJ a tiny smile. She got to her feet. "My trip to Los Angeles was very successful."

DJ froze, her fork halfway to her mouth.

"I have a new position."

"Tell 'em your title," Robert prompted from beside her.

"I am now the district manager in charge of sales."

DJ started to push back her chair.

"The district covers Northern California."

Northern California. We live in Northern California. "I thought the job was in L.A." The words burst out before she could stop them.

"I said the trip was successful. They created a matching position for this area."

DJ let out a whoop and scooped both of the twins up in her arms. They giggled and threw their arms around her neck. "No more changes. You hear that, guys? We're staying right here."

"Right here."

"No changes." The two sounded like parrots.

DJ looked over to see the sun shining on Gran's face. Gran mouthed the words, *I told you so.* "Well, I for one am in favor of no more major changes for this family.

We've had enough challenges lately." She gave Joe that special smile she reserved for him.

"Oh, I don't know about that," Robert said under cover of the hub-bub.

DJ heard him. What kind of changes could he be talking about? Oh-oh. His face was lit with the same kind of smile Gran gave Joe.

Maybe there would be more changes ahead—but then, changes, challenges, both were good. Weren't they?

Coming Winter 1996!

Setting the Pace

Life is settling down to a comfortable pace for DJ Randall when a series of racial slurs aimed at her good friend Hilary cause their jobs at Briones Riding Academy to become nightmares. Will the problems at the Academy hamper DJ's performance in the show ring? Or will the hate messages take on a more violent form? Don't miss Book #3 in the HIGH HURDLES series!